# Permafrost

# BOOKS BY ALASTAIR REYNOLDS

*Revelation Space*
*Chasm City*
*Redemption Ark*
*Absolution Gap*
*Century Rain*
*Pushing Ice*
*The Prefect*
*House of Suns*
*Terminal World*
*Blue Remembered Earth*
*On the Steel Breeze*
*Poseidon's Wake*
*Revenger*
*Elysium Fire*
*The Medusa Chronicles* (with Stephen Baxter)
*Harvest of Time* (Doctor Who)

COLLECTIONS AND ORIGINAL NOVELLAS
*Zima Blue and Other Stories*
*Galactic North*
*Deep Navigation*
*Diamond Dogs, Turquoise Days*
*Beyond the Aquila Rift*
*Slow Bullets*

# PERMAFROST

## ALASTAIR REYNOLDS

A TOM DOHERTY ASSOCIATES BOOK
NEW YORK

PERMAFROST

Copyright © 2019 by Alastair Reynolds

Cover design by Jamie Stafford-Hill
Cover photographs by Tim Robinson/Arcangel Images and mahos/Shutterstock.com

Edited by Jonathan Strahan

A Tor.com Book
Published by Tom Doherty Associates
175 Fifth Avenue
New York, NY 10010

www.tor.com

Tor® is a registered trademark of
Macmillan Publishing Group, LLC.

ISBN 978-1-250-30355-4 (ebook)
ISBN 978-1-250-30356-1 (trade paperback)

First Edition: March 2019

# Permafrost

After I shot Vikram we put our things in the car and drove to the airstrip. Antti was nervous the whole way, knuckles white on the steering wheel, tendons standing out in his neck, eyes searching the road ahead of us. When we arrived at the site he insisted on driving around the perimeter road twice, peering through the security fencing at the hangars, buildings and civilian aircraft.

"You think he's here?"

"More that I want to make sure he isn't." He drove on, leaning forward in his seat, twitchy and anxious as a curb-crawler. "I liked Miguel, I really did. I never wanted it to come to this."

I thought about what we had to do this morning.

"In fairness, you also liked Vikram."

"That took a little time. We didn't click, the two of us, to start with. But that was a long while ago."

"And now?"

"I wish there'd been some other way; any other way." He slowed, steering us onto a side road that led into the private part of the airstrip, at the other end from the low white passenger terminal. "Look, what you had to do back there . . ."

I thought of Vikram, of how he'd followed me out into the field beyond the farm, fully aware of what was coming. I'd taken the artificial larynx with me, just in case there was something he wanted to say at the end. But when I offered it to him he only shook his head, his cataract-clouded eyes seeming to look right through me, out to the grey Russian skies over the farm.

It had taken one shot. The sound of it had echoed back off the buildings. Crows had lifted from a copse of trees nearby, wheeling and cawing in the sky before settling back down, as if a killing was only a minor disturbance in their daily routine.

Afterward, Antti had come out with a spade. We couldn't just leave Vikram lying there in the field.

It hadn't taken long to bury him.

"One of us had to do it," I answered now, wondering if a speck on my sleeve was blood or just dirt from the field.

Antti slowed the car. We went through a security gate and flashed our identification. The guard was on familiar terms with Antti and barely glanced at his credentials. I drew only slightly more interest. "Trusting this old dog to take you up, Miss . . ." He squinted at my name. "Dinova?"

"Tatiana's an old colleague of mine from Novosibirsk," Antti said, shrugging good-humouredly. "Been promising her a spin in the Denali for at least two years."

"Picked a lovely day for it," the guard said, lifting his gaze to the low cloud ceiling.

"Clearer north," Antti said, with a breezy indifference. "Got to maintain my instrument hours, haven't I?"

The guard waved us on. We drove through the gate to the private compound where the light aircraft were stabled. The Denali was a powerful single-engine type, a sleek Cessna with Russian registration and markings. We unloaded our bags and provisions, as well as the airtight alloy case that held the seeds. Antti stowed the items in the rear of the passenger compartment, securing them with elastic webbing. Then he walked around the aircraft, checking its external condition.

"Will this get us all the way?" I asked.

"If they've fuelled it like I requested."

"Otherwise?"

"We'll need to make an intermediate stop, before or after the Ural Mountains. It's not as if I can file an accurate flight plan. My main worry is landing conditions, once we get near the inlet." He helped me aboard the aircraft, putting me in the seat immediately to the left of the pilot's position. My eyes swept the dials and screens, the ranks of old-fashioned switches and knobs. There were dual controls, but none of it meant much to me. "Sit tight, while I go and fake some paperwork."

"And if I see Miguel?"

Covering himself, Antti reached into his leather jacket and extracted the Makarov semiautomatic pistol I'd already used once today. He had already given me a good description of Miguel.

"Make it count, if you have to use it. Whatever Miguel says or does, it's not to be trusted."

He stepped off the plane and went off in the direction of the offices serving the private compound.

*Could you do it, if you had to?*

I brought the automatic out from under my jacket, just enough to see a flash of steel.

*Why not? I did it to Vikram.*

I was glad to see Antti coming back. He had his jacket zipped tight, his arm pressed hard against his side, as if he was carrying a tranche of documents under the jacket. Paperwork, maybe, for when we got to the north. He stooped down to pull away the chocks under the Denali. He got in and started the engine without a word, bringing it to a loud, humming intensity. The propeller was a blur. Almost immediately we were moving off. I didn't need to know much about flying to understand that there was a sequence of procedures, safety checks and so on, that we were ignoring completely.

"Is everything . . ."

The engine noise swelled. It was too loud to talk, and he

hadn't shown me how to use the earphones. I leaned back, trusting that he knew what he was doing. We rumbled onto the strip, gathering momentum. It only took a few seconds to build up to takeoff speed, and then we were up in the air, ascending steeply and curving to the north. Soon the clouds swallowed us. Eventually Antti got us onto something like a level, steady course, ploughing through that grey nothingness. He reduced the power, adjusted our trim and tapped a few commands into the GPS device mounted above the instrumentation.

Only then did he take the time to plug in my earphones and select the intercom channel.

"You can put the gun away. We won't be needing it now."

"What if we run into Miguel, farther north?"

Antti looked at me for a few seconds. It was only then that I saw the stain under his jacket, the wound he'd been applying pressure to when he came back to the plane.

"We won't."

———

Time travel.

More specifically: past-directed time travel.

It was what had taken me from Kogalym in 2080 to that aircraft in 2028, assuming the identity of another woman, ferrying a case of seeds to an uncertain destination in the north, still reeling with the horror of what I had done to Vikram.

Before the plane, though, before the airstrip, before the farmhouse, before the incident in the hospital, there had been my first glimpse of the past. I had been expecting it to happen at some point, but the exact moment that I became time-embedded wasn't easily predictable. No one could say exactly when it would happen, or—with any accuracy—where in the past I would end up.

I was primed, though: mentally prepared to extract the maximum possible information from that first glimpse, no matter how fleeting it would be. The more reference points I could give Cho, the more we understood about the situation—how far back I was, what the host's condition was like, how the noise constraints stood—the better our chances of prolonging further immersions and of achieving our objective.

Which was, not to put it too bluntly, saving the world.

When the glimpse came it was three weeks since I had been moved onto the pilot team, following the bad business with Christos. I'd been there when it went wrong, the catastrophic malfunction in his neural control structure that left him foaming and comatose. The problem was a parasitic code structure that had found its way into his implants. It had always been a danger. Cho had been scraping around for the world's last few samples of viable neural nanotechnology and had been forced to accept that some of those samples might be contaminated or otherwise compromised.

Cho tried to reassure me that I wasn't at risk of the same malfunction, that my implants were civilian-medical in nature and not susceptible to the same vulnerability. They had injected them into me after my stroke, to rebuild the damaged regions of my motor cortex and help me walk again, and now—with a little reprogramming, and a tiny additional surgical procedure—they could be adapted to let me participate in the experiment, becoming time-embedded.

I was on the *Vaymyr*, talking to Margaret as we headed back to our rooms down one of the ice-breaker's metal corridors. Before meeting Margaret in the canteen I'd been in the classroom most of the day, studying archival material—learning all I could about the customs and social structures of the pre-Scouring. Studying computer systems, vehicles, governmental institutions, even foreign languages: anything and everything that might prove useful, even in the smallest way. The other pilots were there as well: Antti, Miguel, Vikram, all of us with our noses pressed to books and screens, trying to squeeze as much knowledge as possible into our skulls, waiting for the moment when we dropped into the past.

Leaning on my stick as I clacked my way down the corridor, I was telling Margaret about Kogalym, sharing my fears that my pupils wouldn't be looked after properly during my absence.

"Nobody thinks it matters anymore," I said. "Education. Giving those girls and boys a chance. And in a way I understand. What's the point, if all they've got to look forward to is gradual starvation or a visit to the mobile euthanisation clinics? But we know. We know there's a chance, even if it's only a small one."

"What did you make of him, Valentina, when Director Cho came to Kogalym?"

"I thought he'd come to take me away, because I'd made an enemy of someone. That's what they do, sometimes—just come in a helicopter and take you away."

"World Health is all we have left," Margaret said, as if this was a justification for their corrupt practices and mob-justice.

"Then he started going on about nutrition, and I didn't know what to think. But at least I knew he wasn't there to punish me." I looked down at Margaret. "Did you know much about him?"

"Only that he was a high-up in World Health, and had

a background in physics. They say he was very driven. The project wouldn't exist without Director Cho. There's a decade of hard work behind all of this, before any of the ships arrived."

"Was he married?"

"Yes, and very happily by all accounts. But she became ill—one of the post-Scouring sicknesses. Director Cho was torn. He wanted to spend time with her, but he knew that the project would falter without his direct involvement. He brought the Brothers together, chose this exact location for the experiment, designed the control structure protocol . . . every detail was under his direct management. But it cost him terribly, not being able to be with his wife in those final months."

"He seems a good man," I said.

If Margaret answered, I didn't hear her.

I was somewhere else.

It was another corridor, but completely different from the metal confines of the ship. There were walls of glazed brick on either side, painted in a two-tone scheme of grey and green. Above was a white ceiling with wide circular lights. Under me was a hard black floor, gleaming as if it had just been polished.

My point of view had swooped down, my eye-level more like a child's. There was a smooth flow of movement on either side, instead of the gently shifting eye-level of a walking gait.

I was being pushed along in a wheelchair, my hands folded in my lap.

Not my hands, exactly: someone else's: still female, but much less wrinkled and age-spotted. Ahead of me—me and whoever was pushing the chair—loomed a pair of red double doors, with circular windows set into them.

Above the doorway was a sign. It said RADIOLOGY. On the double doors were many warning notices.

I stumbled, back in my own body—my own self. Tightened my hand against my cane.

My own, old hand.

"Are you all right?"

"It happened," I said, almost breathless. "It just happened. I was there. I was time-embedded."

"Really?"

"It was a corridor. I was in a wheelchair, being pushed along."

"Are you sure it wasn't a flashback to something that happened to you after your stroke?"

"Totally. I was never in a place like that. Anyway, the hands, her hands . . . they weren't mine. I was in someone else's body."

Margaret clapped in delight. She lifted her head to the ceiling, eyes narrowing behind her glasses. Her fringe fell back from a smooth, childlike brow.

She looked jubilant, transfixed in a moment of pure ecstasy.

"We need to speak to Director Cho. Now. Before you forget the tiniest detail. You've done it, Valentina. The first of any of us. The first person to go back in time."

———

He pressed a button on his intercom, set to one side of his desk, next to a squat, black, military-style telephone. For a habitually neat man, Director Cho's desk was full of technical clutter: bits of machines, instrumentation, disassembled monitors and circuit boards. Despite his administrative role—the one that he had accepted over the care of his ailing wife—he was still an inveterate tinkerer, gifted with restless fingers. When things broke down, it was rumoured to be quicker to send them up to Cho than go through the regular workshops. He would grumble about the imposition on his time, but he still wouldn't be able to resist making something work again.

"I'm piping your testimony through to the *Admiral Nerva*," Cho said. "The Brothers need to hear this. Keep it as clear and concise as you can—you can always add any ancillary detail when you produce your written report." Cho coughed, clearing his voice.

"Brothers, are you listening?"

"We are listening," said the smooth, calm voice of Dmitri.

"I have a testimony from Valentina Lidova. I'm confident she just experienced a few seconds of time-immersion. Visual only. I will ask her to give a brief account of what happened, so that you may begin correlation-matching."

"Please proceed, Miss Lidova," Dmitri said.

Cho slid a microphone over to my side of the desk, its flared base sweeping aside clutter like a snow plough.

I went over what had happened, trying not to embroider any of the details. Margaret had been right to rush me here, with the details still fresh. Cho allowed me to speak without interruption for a minute or two, only breaking in when he could no longer contain himself. I told them what I remembered of the green and grey corridor, the wheelchair, looking down at my own lap.

Next to me, Margaret nodded as I reiterated the details of my experience.

"Skin tone?" Cho asked.

"Pale."

"And are you certain the hands were female?"

"It was just a glimpse, but I'm as sure as I can be." I made a vain attempt at levity. "I don't remember any big hairy knuckles, no anchor tattoos. Aren't we already agreed that you've dropped me into a woman?"

"That's just our best guess, based on imperfect data," Cho said. "Also that we've probably dropped you back around fifty years, give or take—not too far from 2030. You say you were being wheeled into the radiology section, not away from it?"

"It was just a sign over the door. I can't know what they were planning for me once we went through."

"You could read this sign?" Margaret cut in. "It was definitely in Cyrillic?"

"Yes." I had to think for a moment, conscious that the memory of reading something is very distinct from the act itself. But I straightened up, emboldening myself. "There's no doubt. The words were Russian, but in quite an old-fashioned font. It had to be a hospital, somewhere in Russia or a Russian-speaking state."

"Definitely radiology?" Cho pushed.

"What it said over the door."

Alexei's voice came through the intercom. "While we are gratified about the success of the time-embedding, Director Cho, this is nonetheless a concerning development."

Cho took off his round, molelike glasses and rubbed at his scalp. "Yes—it's very worrying. Of course, the flash is a sign that we've had success, and that's good, very good—it means the control structure is embedding, the protocol functioning—but that also means we're entering a period of extreme vulnerability."

"What should Valentina do?" Margaret asked.

"There's not much she can," Cho answered. "Not until she has complete sensorimotor dominance over the host. Until she can walk and talk for herself, she's entirely at the mercy of the people around her. We'll just have to trust that nothing bad happens in the radiology section. Brothers?"

"We are listening," said Ivan.

"If something unfortunate should occur downstream, something that slips through the threshold filters, I don't want Miss Lidova to suffer any upstream consequences. I'd ask you to suspend the link, at least for the next twelve hours. Is that understood?"

Dmitri answered: "The link is now suspended, Director Cho. We will monitor the downstream traffic, nonetheless, and report accordingly."

"Very good," Cho said, moving to switch off the intercom. "We'll reinstate the connection in the morning. In the meantime, Miss Lidova will file her written report."

———————

Beyond the twelve hundred people gathered at the experiment, and a select number of high-level officials beyond it, no one in the world knew that there was a project underway to travel through time.

I'd certainly had no idea, on the day they came to recruit me. The first sign of their approach was a low double-drumming, as their big twin-rotored military helicopter swept in low across the plains around Kogalym. I'd become aware of the sound through the thin walls of the prefab room where I was attempting to conduct a mathematics class. Naturally I'd assumed that the helicopter was there on some other business, nothing that concerned me. I might have ruffled a few feathers in my time, standing up for one child over another, making enemies of this family over that one, but I really wasn't worth the trouble of a visit from the officers of World Health.

So I told myself, until the man came into my classroom.

It was near the end of the hour, so I kept at the lesson, my hand only shaking a little bit. The man was standing at the back, flanked by two guards. He watched me carefully, as if I was being assessed on the quality of my teaching.

Finally the pupils filed out and the man came forward. He sat down at one of the front desks and signalled me to drag a chair over. It was awkward since the chairs were too small and low for either of us, especially my big, burly visitor.

"You are an excellent teacher, Miss Lidova," he said by

way of introduction. "I wish that I'd had you when I was younger. I do not think I would have found Pythagoras quite such a puzzle."

"May I help you, sir?"

"I am Leo Cho," he said, settling his hands before him. "Director of World Health." He had a soft voice despite his large frame, and his hands were long-fingered and delicate-looking, as if they might have belonged to a surgeon or pianist. "I've come to Kogalym because I believe you might be of assistance to me."

"I'm not sure how I can be," I said, with due deference.

"Let me be the judge of that." He was not Russian; Chinese perhaps, but he spoke our language very well indeed, almost too meticulously to pass as a true native speaker. It was no longer unusual to have foreigners active in regional administration: since the Scouring, World Health had been moving its senior operatives around with little regard for former national boundaries. What was the point of countries, when civilisation was only a generation away from total extinction? "What I have," Cho continued, "is a proposition—a job offer, so to speak."

I looked around the classroom, trying to see it from a stranger's point of view. There were geometry diagrams, and pictures of famous mathematical and scientific figures from history, but also odd personal touches, like the chart showing different kinds of butterflies and moths, and another with a huge photomicrograph of a wasp's compound eye.

"I already have one, sir."

He nodded back at the door that the pupils had just slouched through. "What would you say is the main difficulty facing those children, Miss Lidova?"

I didn't have to think very hard about that.

"Nutrition."

Cho gave a nod, seemingly pleased with my answer. "I'm in complete agreement. They're all half-starved. We adults can put up with it, but children are developing individuals. These hardships are damaging an entire generation."

"It'd be a problem," I answered in a low voice, "if there was any worry of there being another generation."

"Things are admittedly quite difficult." He took a slip of grubby, folded-over paper out of his shirt pocket, holding it between his fingers like a single playing card. I expected him to show me whatever was on the paper, but he just held it there like a private talisman. "No suitable seed stocks came through the Scouring unscathed. The national and international seed vaults were supposed to be our hedge against global catastrophe, but one by one they failed, or were destroyed, or pillaged. Those that survived did not contain the particular seeds we require. Now we are down to a few impoverished gene stocks. Nothing will take, nothing will grow—not in the new conditions. Hence, we're digging into stored rations, which will soon be depleted."

I felt a chill run through me.

"World Health isn't usually so frank."

"I can afford frankness. We've located some genetically modified seeds which we think will do very well, even in virtually sterile soil. We only need a sample of them for our production agronomists to work with; they can then clone and distribute the seeds to World Health sites in the necessary quantities." He tapped the grubby paper against the table. "I've studied your career. You have shown great dedication and commitment to your pupils. This is your chance to really help them, by assisting in the effort to safeguard these samples."

I smiled apologetically at him, feeling a vague sense of embarrassment, a feeling that I'd wasted his time, even though it was no fault of my own.

"You've got the wrong Valentina Lidova."

"Your mother was the mathematician Luba Lidova?"

"Yes," I answered, taken aback.

Cho nodded. "Then I am fairly sure I have the right one."

Antti was right about the cloud cover. After an hour's flight—nowhere near the range limit of the Cessna Denali—we broke through into clearer skies. Ahead, cresting the horizon, was a brown line of hills, very sharply defined. The GPS device above the instrument panel showed a coloured trace with our planned trajectory. Antti's eyes switched between the device and the dials and lights on the main console. We were flying a few degrees east of due north, heading into colder air and an eventual meeting with the waters of the Yenisei Gulf, still more than a thousand kilometres beyond us.

He'd said almost nothing since we lifted from the airstrip.

"Are you going to be all right?" I asked, trying to break through his silence.

"Worry about yourself. I'm not the one who had to put a gun to Vikram."

I'd been pushing the memory of that as far back as it would go, but Antti's words brought back the event with a shocking clarity, as if strobe flashes were going off in my head. The cold of the fields, the smell of the gun, the crows wheeling the sky, the whimper and exhalation as Vikram went down, taking a few ragged breaths before his last moment.

"It had to be done," I said, as if that would make it right. "Do you want to tell me what happened back at the airstrip?"

"Miguel was there."

"Yes, I worked that out for myself."

"He had a knife, not a gun. I suppose he was worried about creating too much commotion, getting caught afterward, and the paradox noise he'd be sending up the line. A knife was much simpler." Antti shifted in the pilot's position, suppressing a groan of discomfort. "He got me, but not too deeply. Nicked a rib, maybe. I don't think he hit anything vital. I was ready, and I got the knife off him."

"Then there's a body back at the airstrip. Which someone's bound to have discovered by now."

"There's a reason I don't have the radio and transponder switched on," Antti said. "All they'll be trying to do is persuade us to turn back. Still, there's not much the authorities can do now. I hope to have thrown them off the scent with the flight plan, but even if they work out that we're going north, we're too fast for anything to get ahead of us."

There were two levels of difficulty facing us. Hostile operatives, like Miguel, who were trying to act against the interests of Permafrost, and the local authorities, who could cause nearly as much trouble just by doing their jobs.

"They might radio ahead, get someone on the ground waiting for us?"

"There'll be too many possible landing points to cover.

A few hours' grace is all we need, just enough to get the seeds to safety." He glanced at me, tension etched into his facial muscles. "We'll be all right."

"What do you think got into Miguel?"

He flew on in silence for a few moments, pondering my question. "We'd have had to ask him. But I think it must be the same thing that got into Vikram, near the end. There's something else trying to get into our heads, something else trying to take over our control structures. I've felt it, too. Glimpses, like the first flashes we had going back."

"Tell me about these flashes, Antti."

"Glimpses is all they are. I think there's something going on farther upstream, beyond Permafrost, beyond what we know of the *Vaymyr* and the *Admiral Nerva*. Beyond the whole experiment, beyond 2080. Vikram had visions."

I almost hesitated to ask him, not certain I cared to know the answer.

"What kind?"

"Whiteness. White sky, white land. Machines as big as mountains, floating over everything. Blank white skyscrapers, like squared-off clouds. Nothing else. No people. No cities. No trace that we were ever here, that we ever existed."

"We started something really bad."

"A box of snakes," Antti said, tilting the control stick as we made a course adjustment, following the glowing thread on the GPS screen. "But then, don't blame Cho for any of this. He was only ever following the trail of crumbs your mother threw down."

I thought of my mother still being out there, the telephone call, the long silences as she processed the unfamiliar voice on the end of the line. Wondering now if she believed a word of it, or if I'd only succeeded in driving the spike further into her heart.

———

In the morning after my first glimpse of the hospital corridor—the wheelchair and the radiology sign—Cho and I went to speak to the Brothers. There was a direct line from Cho's office, allowing voice, video and data-transfer, but sometimes it was quicker and easier to speak to them directly. It required a trip across the connecting bridge from the *Vaymyr* to the *Admiral Nerva*, then a long walk into the dark bowels of the aircraft carrier, beneath the main hangar deck where we maintained the time-probes.

As we approached them the Brothers gave off a low, powerful humming, like a sustained organ note. Cho had his chin lifted and his hands behind his back, appearing meek and schoolboyish, despite his large stature.

Each Brother was a black cylinder two metres tall and about fifty centimetres in diameter, with a glossy outer casing. The floor around each cylinder was made up of grilled plates that could be lifted up for access. Beneath the Brothers was a glowing root-system of electronics, refrigeration circuits and fibre-optic connections, spreading invisibly far beneath our feet.

"Good morning," Cho said.

"Good morning, Director," responded Dmitri, the nearest of the machines. "We trust you slept well last night?"

"I did, besides being a little concerned about the welfare of our host."

Pavel asked: "What was your specific concern, Director Cho?"

"Valentina—Miss Lidova—had a clear glimpse of a hospital corridor, leading to a radiological department. It may well be part of the Izhevsk facility, given what we know of time-probe eighteen's history, but it's a little too soon to rule out the other two possible locations. We'll hope to have a better idea with a deeper immersion. Before I risk sending her back in again, though, I want a categorical assurance that the host has suffered no ill effects due to anything that might have happened in that radiology section."

"We are detecting normal neural traffic, Director Cho."

"I'll need more than that, Ivan."

The Brothers were artificial intelligences, each the most powerful and flexible such machine that could be provided by four of the main partners in the Permafrost enterprise. They all predated the Scouring—nothing like them could be made anymore—and although they might look identical now, each was based on a very different logical architecture. Once installed in the *Admiral Nerva,* and arranged to work as a committee, the machines had been shrouded in these anonymising casings and given new designations. They were Dmitri, Ivan, Alexei and Pavel, after *The Brothers Karamazov.*

It was the Brothers who listened to the time-probes, sensing their quantum states and histories, and deciding when a time injection was viable, as well as interpreting the flow of data coming upstream once an injection had been achieved. No human being could do that, nor any simple computer system, and the collective analysis was already pushing the Brothers to the limit of their processing ability.

"There is no sign of neurological impairment," Alexei stated, with a definite firmness of tone. "We cannot model a complete sensorium-mapping for the downstream control structure, but all parameter states indicate that it is safe to reinstate Miss Lidova."

This was the central difficulty with the control structures. They could grow in our heads, allowing neural traffic to flow from upstream to downstream, from pilot to host—and back again, for control and monitoring purposes. Or, in my case, be reprogrammed from an existing set of neural implants. But the way the structures adapted and modified themselves was inherently unpredictable. It took one human mind to make sense of the data flowing from another. The Brothers could eavesdrop on the data, they could optimise the signal and quantify it according to certain schemata, but we wouldn't be able to tell what had really happened to my host until I was inside her skull, looking out through her eyes.

Cho looked at me. "I wish there could be better guarantees than that. I won't force you back if you feel unprepared. Even after what happened to Christos, even if you were the last pilot, I would insist that this is voluntary."

I remembered Christos going into convulsions two weeks after his control structure had been activated. We'd been in the canteen together, pilots and technical experts bonding over coffee and cards. Christos hadn't had a glimpse at that point, but we all felt that he must be on the verge; that it could only be a matter of days before he went time-embedded. No hint, even then, that I was going to be the one to take his place.

Me, a seventy-one-year-old woman, a lame mathematician from Kogalym, a widow despised by half her community for trying to be a good teacher?

Me, the first person to travel in time?

"Send me back in," I said.

———————

After speaking to the Brothers we returned to the *Vaymyr*. Cho waited until I'd had breakfast with Vikram, Miguel and Antti, and then asked for the link to be reinstated. Then it was just a matter of time, waiting for our twinned control structures to mesh again, as they had during that brief flash in the corridor. It couldn't be predicted or rushed.

Cho wanted to have me under close observation, so I was strapped into the dental chair while Dr. Abramik and the other technicians set up their monitoring gear. Margaret's team was handling the signal acquisition and processing hardware; Abramik's people the biomedical systems. There were lots of screens, lots of traces and graphs. They even had pen recorders running, twitching out traces onto paper, just in case there was a power-drop and the electronic data was lost or corrupted.

"We'll hope for a deeper immersion," Cho said. "Get what you can—any details, no matter how trivial. But the moment you feel like you're not in control, or the situation is too complicated for you to act plausibly, issue the abort command. I'd rather pull you out early than run into paradox noise. Is that understood?"

"Understood."

"Then good luck, Miss Lidova."

---

I waited and waited. It wasn't like trying to fall asleep, or drift into a trance. My internal mental state didn't matter at all. Stillness was the only real prerequisite, to reduce the neural traffic burden to a manageable level during these early stages. Given that it had taken weeks for me to have the first glimpse, there was a strong chance that it might not happen at all today, or indeed for many days. But I felt confident that it would happen more readily the second time, and that with each occurrence it would become easier to induce the next.

Eventually—an hour or so after I climbed into the chair—it clicked.

As before, there was no warning. Just a sharp transition in my visual input—switching from the signals in my optic nerves to those in hers, intercepted and translated by the control structures.

I found myself in a room this time, not a corridor. I was reclining, but more fully than in the dental chair. I was in a bed, lying nearly horizontal but with my head propped up against pillows.

I could feel them. I'd been a disembodied presence during the first glimpse, seeing but not experiencing, but now there was a tactile component to the immersion. I registered a soft enclosing pressure around the back of my neck, as well as a faint scratchiness, not quite sharp enough to count as discomfort. Excited by this new level of sensory detail, I made an unconscious effort to alter the angle of my gaze. More of the room came into view, but out of focus, as if through foggy glass.

It was a hospital room. To the left was a wall with an outside window, blinds drawn and angled slightly to deflect daylight. In front of me, beyond the foot of the bed, was a blank wall with a blank rectangular screen attached via an angled bracket. To my right was a partition wall containing a door and a curtained window, which must face out into a corridor or ward.

I swivelled my gaze a bit more, moving her entire head. I felt a variation in the scratchiness, my head shifting on the pillow. Bedside cabinets to the left and right. A chair with padding coming out of its fabric. A fire extinguisher by the door.

Now came an auditory impression. It must have been there all along, but I was only now processing it. Low voices, coming from the other side of the door. Footsteps, doors opening and closing. Beeps and electronic tones. Telephone sounds, hospital noises. The ordinary, busy clamour of a large institution. It could be a school, a government building, our own project. It didn't sound like the past.

I was able to move my head, so I tried my right arm. It responded, even if it felt as if I were trying to push my way through treacle. I lifted it as high as I could go. My sleeve fell back, exposing skin nearly all the way to the elbow joint. I spread her fingers, marvelling at the supreme strangeness of this moment. Whoever my host was, she was definitely younger than me, and all skin and bone.

We knew almost nothing about her, except that she was female. Even that was uncertain. When we dropped the initiating spore into her head via the time-probe, before the spore began to extend itself into a functioning control structure, the spore had run some basic biochemical tests on its immediate environment, and then sent the results of those tests back up to the present using the Luba Pair. The tests had indicated female blood chemistry, but it would have to wait until I was in the body before we had definite verification of gender, ethnicity, age and so forth.

A plastic bracelet had been fixed around the wrist. I twisted the hand, bringing a plastic window into view with printed details beneath it. Even though the room was out of focus, I could read the label quite easily. It said:

T. DINOVA.

Growing more confident in my control, I inspected both arms for signs of surgical monitors or drip-lines, just in case I was wired into some machine or monitor. But there was nothing. Cautiously, I pushed myself a bit higher in the bed. There was a tray in front of me, resting on a table that had been wheeled across the bed from one side. On the tray was a mostly finished meal, with a plate sitting under a transparent plastic heat-cover and a knife and fork set on the plate. I stared at the food for a few seconds, wondering how it compared with our rations, even the improved rations at the station. Somewhere in this hospital, I thought, there would be a huge, bustling kitchen where thousands of meals were prepared each day, where food was made and food wasted, and no one really cared.

Still, at least my host must have had an appetite.

I reached back with my left hand to explore my scalp. I found a bandage, quite a heavy one, but no wires or tubes.

There wasn't anything to stop me from getting out of bed.

I felt I owed it to Cho to try. I had to give him something more than a scrap of a name. I folded back the sheets, gaining—it seemed to me—a little more fluency with each action.

I had on a hospital gown and nothing else. I swung my bare legs out of bed, steadying myself with both hands, then planted my feet on the floor. Cold. I smelled something, as well: a musty tang that clung to me as I pushed my way off the bed.

Me. My own unwashed self.

I tried to stand.

I pushed myself up, right hand against the bed, left using the bedside cabinet as a support. My knees were weak under me, but after using a cane for fifteen years I was accustomed to a certain unsteadiness. I risked a step in the direction of the window, deciding that it was my best option for immediate orientation. I made one unsteady footfall, my vision still not fully in focus, my head feeling swollen and top-heavy. But I was upright. I took another step, arms wide like a zombie tightrope-walker. Two more paces and I'd reached the window, grasping for the temporary support of the sill.

I paused to catch my breath and wait for a wave of dizziness to pass.

She must have been feeling me. That was a given, if she was conscious. Her eyes were open when I dropped into her, so she must have been at least semi-awake. And then her body started doing things on its own. How frightening that must have seemed. She could still see through her own eyes, still experience sounds and impressions, but the control was mine. I decided what she did and what she looked at.

"I'm sorry," I tried to say. "I promise this is only temporary."

A mush of slurred syllables spilled from my mouth.

"Sorry," I tried again, concentrating on that one word in the hope that some part of it might get through.

Still, I had more immediate and pressing issues than this woman's mental well-being. I used my free hand to fumble at the drawstring. The dusty plastic blinds started to click toward the ceiling, and I gained my first fuzzy impression of the world beyond this room.

Out of focus, still. But enough to be going on with. I was several floors up, looking down on a courtyard flanked by what must be two wings of the hospital, extending out from the part of the building containing my room. All concrete, metal and glass. If the layout of the wings was any guide, I had to be on the sixth floor of an eight-storey building.

What else could I give Cho? In the courtyard, paths wound their way around an ornamental pond. Farther out, there was a service road and some parked vehicles, glinting in sunshine, and beyond that some outlying buildings. The ground shadows were attenuated. I couldn't see the sun, but it had to be quite high up in the sky.

I glanced back at the bedside cabinet and made out the silvery squiggle of a pair of glasses.

Cho had told me that even the smallest detail could help with locating my position, even something as innocuous as a vehicle registration number. Suitably determined, I started my return to the bedside. I'd only taken a couple of steps when there was a polite tap on the door. A moment later it swung open and a white-coated young man stepped in from the space beyond the partition wall.

*Get out of me.*

My knees buckled. I started to stumble. The young doctor looked at me for an instant, then sprang in my direction. He'd been carrying a sheath of papers, which he tossed onto the bed to free his hands. I felt him catch me just before I went over completely. For a second, ludicrously, we were posed like a pair of ballroom dancers, me swooning into his embrace.

I took him in. Twenties, fresh-faced, a dusting of youthful stubble, but just enough tiredness around the eyes to suggest a junior doctor's workload.

"What are you playing at, Tatiana?" he said, in perfectly good and clear Russian. "You're barely out of surgery, and already trying to break your neck?"

I looked at him. I wanted to reply, wanted to give him an answer that would satisfy his curiosity, but I wasn't ready.

*What are you waiting for?*

"Permafrost," I whispered, repeating the word twice more.

———————

Cho had come back to Kogalym two days after our meeting in the school. He'd been south on some business.

"Very good, Miss Lidova!" he said, shouting above the engine noise. "I am so glad you will be joining us!"

I had to shout in reply.

"You promise me the pupils will be well looked after?"

"The arrangements are already in place—I've spoken to all the local administrators and made sure that they understand what needs to be done." His gaze settled onto my surly-faced porter, the man who'd been deputised to help with my baggage and books. "That is properly understood, Mr. Evmenov? I'll hold you personally accountable if there's any lapse in the provisions." Cho beckoned me aboard. "Quickly, please. We don't want to lose our weather window."

I went up the ramp, stooping to avoid denting my head on the overhang. My cane thumped on the metal floor. I had to squeeze past some hefty item occupying most of the helicopter's cargo section. It was the size of a small truck and covered in sheets. It didn't have the shape of a truck, though. More a turbine or aircraft engine: something large and cylindrical. Or a piece of genetics equipment: some industrial unit recovered from an abandoned university or industrial plant.

"What is that thing, Mister Cho?" I asked, as I was shown to my seat just behind the cockpit, on the right side of the helicopter. "A gene synthesizer, for your seed program?"

As he buckled in opposite me, Cho considered my question, tilting his head slightly to one side. It meant that he was searching for an answer that was close to the truth, while not being the thing itself.

"It does have a medical application, yes."

The engine surged and the rotors dragged us into the air. We were soon flying north from Kogalym. We passed over a scattering of ghost towns and villages, no lights showing from their empty buildings. The terrain was getting icier with each kilometre we covered.

After a few hours we touched down near an isolated military compound. Cho asked me if I wanted to stretch my legs; I declined. Cho got out and stood around while some trucks came out to meet us. Hoses were connected and fuel began to gurgle in. Another truck came, this time with a flatbed. Some boxes were unpacked and driven away. Cho got back aboard and we fought our way back into the air.

"We were a little heavy," Cho said, turning to address me across the narrow aisle. "We had to unload some nonessential supplies, or we wouldn't have made it between fuel stops." He waved his fingers. "It's nothing to worry about."

We continued into darkness. There were no lights out there at all now. Every now and then the helicopter would put out a searchlight and I'd be surprised at how high or low we were.

"How far north are we going, Director?"

"To the Yenisei Gulf. It's a little remote, but it turned out that it was the best place to locate our project. We needed somewhere with maritime access, in any case."

"Something to do with your seeds? A genetics lab?"

Cho reached into a pouch behind the pilot's position. He drew out a document and passed it to me. It was a scarlet brochure, with a translucent plastic cover. On the front was the World Health logo, followed by a statement in several languages to the effect that the contents were of the highest security rating.

I looked at him doubtfully, before I opened the document.

"Go ahead," Cho said. "You're committed now."

I opened the document.

On the inside page was a logo. It was a six-armed snowflake with three letters in the middle of it.

The letters were:

PRE

I turned over to the next page. It was blank except for three words in Russian:

Permafrost Retrocausal Experiment

I looked at Cho, but his expression gave nothing away. Behind his round-rimmed glasses, his eyes were sharply observant but betraying nothing more.

Once again, I felt as if I was under assessment.

I turned to the next page. There was a very short paragraph, again in Russian.

The Permafrost Retrocausal Experiment aims to use Luba Pairs to achieve past-directed time travel.

I turned to the next page. It became very technical very quickly. There was talk of time-injection, time-probes, Luba Pairs, Lidova noise, grandfathering.

Interspersed with the text were graphs and equations. Some of them I recognised well enough from my mother's papers, but there were also aspects well outside my own limited expertise, or perhaps recollection.

I went all the way through the document, then turned back to the prefacing paragraph to make sure I wasn't going mad.

It seemed that I wasn't.

We flew on for a few more minutes. I debated with myself what to say, and how I might say it. Perhaps it was all still a test, to gauge the limits of my credulity. How stupid would I need to be, to think that any of this was real?

But Cho did not seem like a man predisposed to frivolity.

"You're attempting time travel."

"We're not attempting it," Cho answered carefully.

"Of course not."

"We've already achieved it."

———

The sound of engines always made me drowsy. I was daydreaming of being back in Cho's helicopter, thinking of the first time I'd seen the lights of Permafrost, when a shrill beep pulled me back into Antti's Cessna. It was the GPS system, alerting us to something. I turned to Antti, expecting him to respond to the notification, but his head was slumped, his chin lolling onto his collar, his eyes slitted. The GPS alert didn't sound urgent enough to mean that anything was seriously wrong with the plane, but it must have meant that we'd arrived at some waypoint, some moment in our journey when my companion was supposed to take action.

"Antti," I said.

The plane carried on. The beeping continued. I called out his name again, and when that didn't work I jabbed him in the ribs with my elbow, avoiding the area on the right side of his chest where he'd been wounded. Antti grunted, and shuddered back to consciousness. There was a second of fogginess, then he took action, adjusting the controls and flicking switches, until the twin alarms eventually silenced.

"It was nothing. I just dozed off for a second or two."

"You were out cold." I reached out and touched the back of my hand against his forehead. "You're clammy. What the hell happened back there?"

Antti managed a self-effacing smile. "Maybe he got me a bit deeper than I thought. Nicked more than a rib."

"You need a hospital. It could be anything: internal bleeding, organ damage, infection. There are still some towns ahead of us. Get us down now, while you're still able to land safely."

"I'm all right," Antti said, straightening up in the seat. "I can do this. We can do this. We have to get to the Yenisei Gulf."

I nodded, desperately wanting to believe him. What other option did I have? But that tiredness was already showing in his eyes again.

---

It began as a glimmer of yellow and blue lights on the horizon, casting a pastel radiance on the low-lying clouds over the station. The helicopter came in closer, dropping altitude. The lights were arranged in a flattened circle, like a coin seen nearly edge-on, a makeshift community of labs and offices staked down on frozen ground, with a sharp enclosing boundary, like a medieval encampment.

So I thought.

Closer still. There was flat ice under us now: not frozen ground, but frozen water. Gently rising ground to either side of this tongue of ice, the compound built entirely on the flat part.

It was a river, or an inlet, completely frozen.

The enclosing shield was not continuous, I realised. It was made up of the hulls of ships: numerous slab-sided vessels gathered in a ringlike formation. The lights were coming from their superstructures. That was all it was: lots of ships, gathered together, some forming a ring and others contained within it, with one very large ship in the middle.

Cho looked at me, waiting for a reaction, something in his manner suggesting a quiet pride.

I decided to let him speak.

"We had need of secrecy, as well as isolation from

sources of electrical and acoustic noise," he explained. "We also had to be largely independent, with our own power supply. In the end, the most practical solution was to base our experiment around these ships. They were sailed into this inlet when the waters were still navigable, before the freeze got really bad."

We circled the perimeter. There were ships of all shapes and sizes. A small majority were obviously ex-military, but there were also cargo ships and some with cranes or heavy industrial equipment on their decks. A medium-sized cruise liner, a passenger ferry, a few tugs, even a submarine, only the upper part of it showing above the ice.

Cho pointed out the names of some of the ships. "That is the *Vaymyr,* where you will spend most of your time. That is the *Nunivak,* where we have our heavy workshops. That is the *Wedell* . . ."

By far the largest ship, though, was an aircraft carrier.

"That is the hub of our experiment," Cho said. "The *Admiral Nerva.* Ex–Indian Navy, fully nuclear. It's where we've gathered the time-probes, the devices we use to inject matter into the past. They've very sensitive to interference, so there are only ever a small number of technicians allowed on the *Nerva.*"

"These probes are time machines? Time machines that you've built, and actually got to work?"

"To a degree."

"You said you'd done it."

"We have—but not as well, or as reliably, as we'd wish."

We picked up height to get over the cordon. There were no other helicopters flying around, although I did see another one parked on the back of one of the ships. All the ships were interconnected, strung together by cables and bridges, some of which were quite sturdy looking and others not much better than rope-ways. Since the decks were all at different levels, the bridges were either sloped or went into the sides of the hulls, through doors that must have been cut into them just for Permafrost. There were also doors down on the level of the ice, and some tracks in the ice marked by lanterns. I spotted a tractor labouring between two of the ships, dragging some huge, sheeted thing behind it on a sort of sledge.

We began to descend. There was a landing pad under us, on the back of a squat, upright-looking ship with a disproportionately tall superstructure.

"This is the *Vaymyr*," Cho said. "One of our key vessels. It supplies a large fraction of our power budget, but it also serves as our main administrative centre. My offices are in the *Vaymyr*, as well as several laboratories, kitchens, recreational areas and your own personal quarters, which I hope will be to your satisfaction. You'll meet the pilots very shortly, and I think you'll get on very well with them. They'll be grateful for your expertise."

"Pilots?"

"I ought to say prospective pilots. They'll be the ones who go into time, when the experiment's problems are ironed out. But as yet none of them have gone back. We are close, though. There are no longer any fundamental obstacles. It's largely the final question of paradox noise that's causing us difficulties."

"I think you may be expecting too much of me."

"I doubt it very much," Cho answered.

———

He asked me why I had been so quick to issue the abort phrase, just when we were getting somewhere.

"The young doctor was talking to her, and I knew I wasn't going to be able to respond properly."

"Why was that an immediate difficulty?"

"She's in hospital, and she's just had something done to her head. If she starts not being able to speak properly, they may think something's very wrong with her, and then order a follow-up test. I didn't want to take that chance, in case they take her back to the radiology department."

"We still don't really know what happened, between

your first and second episodes. Clearly there was no last-ing damage."

"Maybe they never put her in the scanner that time. There are other things in radiology departments besides MRI machines."

"That's possible," allowed Abramik, who was sitting in on the interrogation/debrief. "An X-ray, for instance, or even a CT scan. But you have a name for us, at least."

"Tatiana Dinova," I answered.

Cho reached over desktop clutter to switch on his intercom again. "Brothers. Run a search on a possible host subject named Tatiana Dinova." His eyes flicked to me. "Under forty at the time of the immersion?"

I thought of her hands, how young they'd looked compared to my own.

"Probably."

"No unusual spelling?"

"I saw the surname written down, but only heard the doctor mention her given name. Dinova. D-I-N-O-V-A. You'd better try variant spellings of Tatiana, just in case."

"We shall," said Dmitri through the intercom speaker. "Does Miss Lidova have any other parameters that may be useful?"

"It was before the Scouring," I said. "That much I'm sure of. A big hospital with about eight floors, with wings stretching out from a central block. It didn't look like winter to me. I think we were farther south than Koga-lym, but still in Russia."

"Time-probe eighteen was only active at three loca-tions before it came into Director Cho's possession," said Pavel, who had the highest-sounding voice of the Broth-ers. "One of these was a military institution in Poland, so that may be discarded on the basis of Miss Lidova's testi-mony."

"I was in Russia," I affirmed. "The signs were in Russ-ian, the doctor spoke Russian. What are the other two places?"

"Two institutions," said Ivan, who had the deepest and slowest voice of the four. "Both west of the Ural Moun-tains. One is a private medical facility in Yaroslavl, about two hundred kilometres northeast of Moscow. However, the ground-plan and three-storey architecture of this fa-cility does not correspond with Miss Lidova's account. The second facility is more promising. This is the public hospital in Izhevsk, approximately one thousand kilome-tres east of Moscow."

The printer in the corner of Cho's office clicked and whirred to life. A sheet of paper went through it and then slid into the out-tray. Cho wheeled his chair to the printer, collected the paper by his fingertips and returned it to his desk. The paper curled and twitched like some dying marine organism. Cho smoothed it down, using one of his dismantled gadgets, a piece of dial-like instrumentation, as a makeshift paperweight. I leaned over to examine the paper, seeing it upside-down from my perspective.

It was the plan of a hospital, extracted from some civic or architectural database within the Brothers' collective memory.

"That's it," I said, with a giddy sense of recognition. "No doubt about it. I can even see the courtyard and the pond, and the car park beyond the service road. I must have been—must be—in that main block, between the first two wings, looking due north."

"The Izhevsk facility was always a high-likelihood target," Cho said. "But it is good to have this confirmed. Do you have more for us, Brothers?"

"May we assume that the host is present in the Izhevsk facility?" asked Dmitri.

"You may," Cho said.

"Then the injection window must lie between 2022 and 2037, the period in which time-probe eighteen was installed and active in Izhevsk," Dmitri replied. "We are retrieving patient records for that hospital, as well as civil documents for the greater Izhevsk region."

"Who is she?" I asked, prickling with anticipation. I knew it wouldn't take them long to sift their memories.

"We have identified Tatiana Dinova," said Ivan. "Would

you like a biographical summary, Director Cho?"

Cho nodded. "Send it through."

His printer began again. The life of a woman, almost certainly long dead, began to spool into the out-tray. Tatiana Dinova, whoever she was. *My* Tatiana Dinova.

My host: my means of altering the past.

"You'll have to convince them you're well enough to be discharged," Abramik said, stroking the tip of his beard. "I can help you with some neurological pointers, if you start being questioned. But in the meantime, we'll need a contingency plan—a fallback in case they try to bring you back to the radiology section." He turned to Cho. "Could we risk limited sabotage of the probe, if Valentina got close enough to it?"

"Provided it *was* limited. If she damages the machine beyond repair, we'll be in quite a lot of trouble."

"It wouldn't need to be that bad," Abramik said. "There'll be an emergency control somewhere nearby, probably on a wall or under a hinged cover. It's what they'd use if there was a problem during a scan: dumps the helium from the magnets, lets them warm up and lose their superconducting current. It's quicker and safer than just cutting the power. All she'd need to do is reach that control, and she'd have the element of surprise. The one thing they won't be expecting is that."

"We could risk erasing the probe's quantum memory,"

Margaret countered. "Those magnets can't go through too many warm-up cycles before they cease being traversable by Luba Pairs."

"Then something not *quite* as drastic," Abramik said, flashing an irritated look at the physicist, as if she were being deliberately obstructive, rather than raising an entirely reasonable concern. "Smuggle a metal object into the room, something ferromagnetic, keep it hidden until the last moment. If we're lucky, it'll be attracted to the machine before the field has a chance to do any lasting damage to the control structure."

"If Tatiana's lucky, you mean," I said.

———

My first evening at Permafrost was like any first time at a large, unfamiliar institution. I'd been wrenched from the small, settled world of a provincial teacher and thrown into a busy, complex environment full of new faces and protocols. In a well-meaning way, Cho was trying to spoon as much information as possible into me as we went to my quarters, up a couple of flights of stairs inside the icebreaker *Vaymyr*. He was explaining emergency drills, power cuts, medical arrangements, mealtimes, social gatherings, pointing this way and that as if I could see through grey metal walls to the rooms and ships beyond, and as if I had a hope of remembering half of it. Eventually I stopped listening, knowing that it would all fall into place in its own time.

"You may well wish to unwind after our journey," Cho was saying as we reached my room. "But if I could impose on you a little longer, it would be very good to meet the pilots as soon as possible." He lifted a sleeve to glance at his watch. "If we are lucky, they will still be in the canteen."

"Give me a minute," I said.

While Cho waited at the door to my room I tidied away my bag then stripped down to a sweater and a shirt, much as I would have worn during classroom hours. I went to the basin and splashed some water on my face, a token effort at freshening up after the helicopter flight. I looked tired, old. Not ready for a new adventure, but rather someone who'd already been through too many in one life.

I stepped out of the room, locking it with the key I'd been given.

"Tell me about the pilots."

"Our four prospective time travellers. You'll be working closely with them as we deal with the remaining obstacles."

I thought of the scale and probable expense of this operation.

"Just four, after all the trouble you've gone to?"

"I would gladly wish for more. But we are limited by factors outside our control, including our access to neural nanotechnology." For a moment Cho, too, showed something of the strain life had put on him. "Such things are in very short supply these days, and we've had to fight hard to consolidate what we have. That is true of the project as a whole, from our secondhand ships to the time-probes themselves. Everything is make-do-and-mend, and we cannot be too choosy." But he flashed an encouraging smile. "What we can be is resourceful and adaptable—and I think we have been."

The canteen was quiet, except for a small group at one of the tables near a main window. They were leaning into each other, engaged in low, urgent conversation. Young and early-middle-aged people, men and women both, a blend of accents. Remains of food on their trays, half-finished drinks, beer bottles, a pack of cards, a paperback book. There was no chance that this little room was capable of providing for twelve hundred people, even with staggered shifts, so I guessed this was what amounted to the VIP dining area.

Cho knocked on the serving hatch and got them to open up for us.

"It's still dried or frozen food, for the most part," he said. "But we are very fortunate in having the pick of the available rations flown in for us, from all areas of World

Health. They've been made to understand the importance of our effort, if not its precise nature."

Once we'd gotten our food he steered me to the table where the other people were seated.

"That said, we work like dogs." He pulled out a seat for me, while balancing his tray single-handedly. "There are twelve hundred people stationed here at Permafrost, all exceptional individuals. All valued. But there are fewer than a dozen of us that I would describe as truly irreplaceable—and you are now one of them. We are up against time, Miss Lidova—in all senses. If it takes us ten years to safeguard those seeds, it'll be too late for our food scientists and agronomists to put them to effective use. In fact we have much less time than that. The Brothers tell us that we have about six to nine months to make a difference—a year at the most. After that, we're wasting time. Quite literally."

"The Brothers?"

"Dmitri, Ivan, Alexei and Pavel. *The Brothers Karamazov.* Artificial intelligences, assisting with our endeavour. More make-do-and-mend. They're on the *Nerva,* so you'll meet them eventually." Cho and I took our places, squeezing into orange plastic chairs between the other people. "This is Miss Valentina Lidova," he said, extending a hand to me. "Would you mind introducing yourselves? I assure you she doesn't bite."

A woman leaned over and shook my hand. She had a confident grip. She was about twenty years younger than me, with long black hair and a wide, friendly face, with prominent freckles across the cheekbones.

"I am Antti," she said, speaking slightly accented Russian. "Originally from Finland, one of the pilots." She gave Cho a wary, questioning look. "Does she know, Director?"

"A little," Cho said. He used an opener to work the top off a bottle of beer, and drank directly from the bottle. "You may speak freely, in any case."

"They're trying to send us back in time," Antti said. "Us four pilots. We won't actually go back, really—we'll always be aboard the *Vaymyr*, hooked up to the equipment in the *Admiral Nerva*. We'll just take over hosts in the past, driving their bodies by remote control. That's why they call us pilots. But it'll *feel* like going back, when we're time-embedded."

"If it works," said a handsome, dark-skinned man, hair greying slightly at the temples.

"Of course it'll damn well work," Antti answered. "Why wouldn't it, when the individual steps are all feasible?"

"I am Vikram," said the handsome man, smiling stiffly. "From New Delhi, originally. I hope my Russian isn't too shabby?"

"Oh, stop showing off," Antti said, flashing him an irritated look, as if they were all more than fed up with Vikram's transparent self-deprecation.

"We've sent stuff back," said another man, grinning to lighten the mood, passing me a beer whether I wanted one or not. "Small things, up to about the size of a pollen grain, or an initiating spore of nanotechnology. We know we can do it. It's just a question of putting the final pieces together." He shook my hand. "Christos, from Greece. Or what's left of Greece. Where have you come from, Valentina?"

"Kogalym," I answered. "You won't have heard of it. It's quite a way south, really a nothing sort of place."

"Everywhere is a nothing place soon," said the man next to Christos, who was the only one approaching my own age. Just as well-built as the Greek, but with wrinkles, age spots and mostly silver hair, combed back from his brow. "I am Miguel," he said, speaking Russian but more slowly and stiffly than his comrades. "I am glad they bring you to station." He dropped his voice. "What you know of experiment so far?"

"Director Cho showed me the brochure," I answered truthfully. "Beyond that, almost nothing."

"You'll catch on quickly," said the fifth person at the table, who was a small woman with glasses and a severe black fringe. "I'm Margaret. Margaret Arbetsumian, mathematical physicist."

"Margaret worked on quantum experimental systems before the Scouring," said Cho. "If anyone could turn Luba Lidova's ideas into something practical, I knew it would be Margaret. Miss Lidova could use a rest tonight, Margaret, but in the morning would you care to show her the experimental apparatus—perhaps demonstrate a minimal-case paradox?"

"It'd be my pleasure," Margaret said.

"As for me," said the sixth person at the table, a slender, neatly groomed man with a pointed beard, "what I understand about time travel or paradoxes you could write on the back of a very small napkin. But I do know a thing about physiology, and neuroscience, and nano-therapeutic systems. Dr. Peter Abramik—Peter to my friends." Then he narrowed his eyes, as if sensing the extent of my ignorance. "You really are in the dark about this, aren't you?"

I sipped at my beer and took a few mouthfuls of curry, just to show that I wasn't intimidated by either my new surroundings or my new colleagues. "I'm seventy-one years old," I said, uttering the words as a plain statement of fact, inviting neither pity nor reverence. "The last time I had any serious involvement in my mother's work was fifty years ago, when I was barely into my twenties." I ate a little bit more, purposefully refusing to be hurried. "That said, I've never forgotten it. My mother worked on quantum models for single-particle time travel. She showed how an electron—or anything else, really, provided you could manipulate it, and measure its quantum state—an *electron* could be sent back in time, looped back into the past to become a twin of itself in the future, one half of a Luba Pair. If you manipulated either element of the Luba Pair, the other one responded. You could send signals up and down time. But that was all. You couldn't send back anything much larger than an electron—maybe an atom, a molecule, at the extreme limit, before macroscopic effects collapsed the Luba Pairing. And just as critically, you couldn't observe that time travel had happened. It was like a conjuring trick done in the dark. The moment you tried to observe a Luba Pair in their time-separated state, you got washed out by noise effects."

"Paradox," Margaret said. "Black and white. Either present or absent. If you don't observe, paradox hides its claws. If you attempt to observe, it kills you—metaphorically, mostly."

I nodded. "That's correct."

"But your mother went beyond binary paradox," Cho said. "She developed a whole class of models in which paradox is a noise effect, a parameter with grey values, rather than just black and white."

"She spoke about it less as she got older," I replied. "They hammered her, the whole establishment. Treated her like an idiot. Why the hell should she indulge them anymore?"

"Your mother was correct," Cho said placidly. "This we know. Paradox is inherent in any time-travelling system. But it is containable ... treatable. We have learned that there are classes of paradox, layers of paradox."

Margaret made an encouraging gesture in the direction of Director Cho. "Say it. You know you want to."

Cho reached for his beer, smiling at the invitation. "Paradox itself is ... not entirely paradoxical."

---

The hospital meal service came around. They wheeled the table across my bed, then set out the tray with its plastic cover. I waited until the orderly was out of the room, hid the knife under my pillow, then used the call button to summon them back, before complaining that I didn't have a knife.

It could have gone several ways at that point, but the orderly only shrugged and returned with a fresh knife.

*What are you going to do with that?*

It was a voice in my head. I'd heard it before, during my previous immersion, but it was stronger and clearer now—beyond the point of being ignored.

*You heard me. I asked a question. You're taking me over, at least have the decency to answer it.*

It was Tatiana. I knew it.

I phrased a reply. I didn't need to speak it, just voice the statement aloud in my head.

*You're not supposed to be able to speak to me.*

*And who are you to say what I can and can't do? This is my body, my life. What are you doing in me?*

*Trying to help. Trying to sort out a mess. That's all you have to know.*

I sweated. Me or her, or perhaps both of us. Something was happening with the control structures that was not part of the plan. My host was conscious and communicative, and receiving sensory impressions from upstream.

*Who are you?*

I debated with myself before answering. I had never been very good at lying, and I didn't think I was going to get any better just because I was lying to a voice inside my own head. Worse, perhaps. So I decided that I would be better sticking to the truth, at least a part of it.

*Valentina. I'm . . . a schoolteacher. From an arse-end town called Kogalym. Not a demon, not a witch. But that's all I can tell you, and that's already too much.*

*Are you a hallucination? You don't sound like a hallucination.*

*I'm not. But what I am is . . . look, can we eat your dinner?*

*You need to eat?*

*No. But you do.*

Silence, but only for a few seconds.

*Where are you from, Valentina? Where are you right now, besides being in my head?*

*You wouldn't believe me.*

*Maybe I won't, but you can still answer my question.*

*All right. I'll tell you this much. I'm aboard a ship, an ice-breaker, in northern Russia. I'm in a chair, with doctors and scientists fussing around me. And I'm coming into you from fifty-two years in the future.*

Another silence—longer this time. Nearly enough to make me think she might have gone away for good.

*I'd say you were mad, or lying. Then again, there is a voice in my head, and you have been making me do things. So, for the moment, I'm going to accept this stupid thing you've just told me, because I'd still rather believe you than accept that I'm the mad one.*

*You're not the mad one.*

*Then how about you start by telling me how this is happening? How are you in me?*

*By means of something we put into your head. You were having an MRI scan, and . . . that's how we do it. That's how we reach the past, from 2080. We inject something into your head, a thing about the size of a grain of pollen, and it grows through your brain and lets me take you over, just for a short while.*

*Why?*

*So we can get something done. Something important.*

*And what gives you this right?*

*Nothing. No right at all. But it still has to be done. We're in a mess here, Tatiana, a really bad one, but we can fix things a little by altering the past. Just a tiny amount—not enough to change your life or anyone else's. And after we're done, after you've helped us, you'll never hear from us again. The thing in your brain, the control structure, will self-dismantle. It'll flush itself out of you harmlessly, and you just get on with being you, as if nothing had ever happened.*

She echoed back my words with a cold mockery.

*As if nothing had ever happened. Do you really think it'll be that simple?*

*I do.*

*Then at least you've settled one question for me. I know which one of us is insane.*

───────────

After that, she let me get on with eating in peace and quiet.

Perhaps she'd decided to see if I went away if she stopped interrogating me. That said, it was very definitely me in charge of her as I worked my way through the hospital meal. But exactly how strange would that have felt, anyway? I thought of the times I'd spooned my way through government rations, my mind on the homework I was supposed to be marking, barely conscious of my hand as it went from plate to mouth. There were days when all of us might as well be under the control of disembodied spirits from the future, for all the difference it makes.

Yet this was a screwup, and no mistake. She wasn't supposed to be able to talk to me or hear me in return. It was nothing Cho had ever mentioned as a normal aspect of the control structure functionality. But then again, all of this was experimental. No one had ever linked together two control structures through time, via Luba Pairs.

The meal wasn't bad. I could already smell and taste quite well by then, and it was surprising how full-up I felt by the time I'd emptied the plate. The food wasn't going into my stomach, but the signals from Tatiana's digestive system were still finding their way to my brain, producing the effect of a steadily diminishing appetite.

"We're not bad people," I'd mouthed to myself.

*Then what are you?*

She was back again.

*Please ... for my sake ... for your sake ... just pretend none of this is happening.*

*I wish I could. Trouble is, I keep getting these flashes of double vision. I'm here, and then I'm somewhere else. Not this room. Somewhere without any windows, all metal. I'm in a chair, leaning back, and there are people crowding around. Lots of machines and lights. What is it, some secret government laboratory? Are you testing some way of turning ordinary people into zombies? Putting things in our heads, while we're in hospital? Is that it?*

*Yes. That's exactly it. Mind-control drones. The government's in on it. So's the hospital. And they're reading your mind right now. You're about the tenth subject we've burned through so far. I'd really like to protect you, too, but if you keep talking aloud in your own head, keep asking questions, they're going to pick up on it, and . . .*

*And nothing. You just want me to shut up, is all it is. Still, I think you told me the truth about Kogalym. I had an aunt there once. And you're right, it really is a shit-hole. No one would ever have made that part up.*

---

The one good thing was that sooner or later even Tatiana Dinova had to sleep.

I'd worked out a system with the knife by then, one we'd rehearsed upstream as best we could. If I pushed the admissions bracelet as far up my arm as it would go, I could wedge the handle of the knife under it, with the sharp end digging into the crook of my elbow. It wasn't comfortable, and it relied on my keeping an angle in my arm, but it kept the knife from showing when I let down my sleeve.

The hospital wasn't a restful place at night. There were fewer admissions, the televisions were turned down, and the staff kept their conversations low, but it made very little difference. Electronic monitors still went off at all hours, beeping tones cutting through walls and floors, patients coughed and complained, telephones rang and elevators whined and clattered. Then there were shift changes and people being paged, and fire and security alarms going off in distant wings.

By five the blinds were doing a bad job of masking the arrival of daylight. The doctors were starting their morning rounds. Curtains were being swished back along curving rails. Voices were going up again, the coughs and complaints more full-throated. I reached under the pillow and extracted the knife, then slid it back up my sleeve.

A few minutes before six, the young doctor came into the room, along with an orderly and a vacant wheelchair.

"Good morning, Tatiana. How are we today?"

*Oh, I'm fine. I can't control my body, and there's another voice in my skull, but other than that . . .*

"I'm all right, thank you," I said, speaking aloud for the first time since becoming time-embedded, and forcing out the words as if both our lives depended on it. "Much better than yesterday."

He looked at me for a few seconds. I wondered what was going through his head, the details that were nagging at him. Was my accent and diction consistent with Tatiana Dinova? Was she the sort to say "thank you" at all?

But he smiled and nodded.

"You sound much better. And that confusion you mentioned yesterday—that's all cleared up?"

"No—I'm all right. Whatever that was, it passed."

*I wish you would pass. I was hoping you were a bad dream from last night. But you're sticking around, aren't you?*

The knife was tight against my armpit.

*Just for a little while—yes. I said we've got work to do. But I'm sure we'll get used to each other in time.*

---

On the morning of my first full day at Permafrost, Margaret, Antti and I put on clean-room outfits and then went through a positive-pressure airlock into the *Vaymyr*'s laboratory.

The room was about the size of a large double garage and surgically clean. Positioned on a central bench, surrounded by ancillary equipment and computers, was an upright silver cylinder, about the size of an oil drum. It was festooned with cables and monitors, with telescope-like devices peering into it at various angles.

Margaret went to the device and brought one of the computers to life. Fans whirred. Data and graphs appeared on an array of monitor screens.

"This is how we first created and manipulated a Luba Pair," she said, sounding like a proud parent. "In essence, it's really just a cavity surrounded by a very powerful superconducting magnet. You recall your mother's work on quantum memory states in superconducting systems?"

I nodded in my mask and clean-room hood. "That was when she was beginning to get bounced by the respectable journals."

"That must have been hard for her," Antti said, just her eyes meeting mine over her mask.

We had shared a house since Father died, and my mother had come to depend on me as a sounding board for her wilder ideas, almost as if I were an extension of herself, only a more skeptical, questioning one. That had been flattering to me, when I was in my middle and late teens. To have this celebrated intellect, this world-famous mathematician, treating me as an equal, someone capable of seeing her ideas through fresh eyes, made me feel very special.

But by the time I was approaching my twenties, I knew I had to strike out on my own. I wasn't going to run off and do anything crazy like join a radical arts collective. I still wanted to be a mathematician, but in my own fresh corner of it, a long way away from my mother's crazy work on time-loops and grey paradox.

She took it as a betrayal. Not to my face, not to begin with, but it was always there, simmering. That resentment grew and grew over one long, hot summer, until we had a major bust-up.

Things had never been the same after that.

"Hard on both of us," I said, answering Antti. "All a long time ago, in any case. You're too young to remember what the world was like back then, but it all feels like a different life. I remember the work, though. That's as fresh in my mind as it ever was. All very speculative, even by Mother's standards. But according to her theory, if you were going to attempt to build a time machine, this is where you'd start: with a superconducting system."

"Is the experiment running?" Antti asked.

"Yes, we're in the operating regime," Margaret said. "Luba Pairs are being bred inside the assembly. We're sending electrons back from the future, exactly a minute upstream. They're travelling back sixty seconds, appearing in the magnet, holding coherence for a short while, then becoming noise-limited, which means we can't track the correlation anymore."

It was warm enough in the laboratory, but still I shivered. "This is really happening?"

Antti beckoned me to one of the screens, where a wriggling yellow line was describing a kind of seismic trace. "This is the correlation, summed across multiple Luba Pairs, so that we keep one step ahead of the decoherence effect. It's a signal from the future, so to speak. Our future, one minute ahead of now. It's very noisy in the raw state. We run it through a battery of signal optimisation algorithms drawn from your mother's work, but we're hitting real limits in our understanding of those algorithms, how to make them fit together. The Brothers . . ." She paused, glancing at Margaret. "It's believed we can do much better, with your guidance."

The yellow line jagged upward suddenly, then collapsed back down to its normal noise level. As the spike inched its way to the left, a pair of brackets dropped down on either side of it, accompanied by a set of statistical parameters.

"What was that?" I asked.

"Could be anything," Antti said, with only vague interest. "A noise spike in the upstream electronics, a shift in the ice under the *Vaymyr,* someone dropping a crate on the upper deck. We'll find out in about forty-five seconds, if it's anything at all."

I grinned at their insouciance.

"You're both taking this way too casually."

"We've had lot of time to get used to what we're doing," Margaret said with an apologetic smile, as if they were being bad hosts by not making more of their experiment. "Even time travel becomes normal when it's your day job."

"You constructed this apparatus?" I asked, nodding at the upright cylinder.

"Put it together from parts, more accurately," Margaret said. "But it certainly didn't exist in any significant form until we assembled it here. You're wondering how far back we could have sent those electrons?"

"I'm thinking that a minute doesn't really buy you anything. Time to cheat the stock markets, if there were still stock markets. But not to solve Director Cho's food crisis."

"If we eliminated every source of noise, we could go back fourteen months, the day we first put the apparatus together. Fourteen months would help us in small ways—we could transmit knowledge that would help speed up the development of the experiment, warning us from blind alleys and dead ends. In practise, though, we're nowhere near that. Twelve hours is our effective limit with this setup."

"And on the *Admiral Nerva*?"

"A little further back," Antti said.

I approached the experiment, wanting to get a closer look at the instrumentation. Along the way my cleanroom garment brushed against a pen and clipboard lying on one of adjoining benches. The pen clanged to the floor.

I stared down at it, shaking my head slowly.

"That didn't just happen."

"There's your noise spike," Antti said, stooping down and picking up the pen, then setting it back on the bench as if this was a completely mundane happening. "Congratulations, Valentina. You just made a small alteration to the past."

I looked at Margaret's apparatus, thinking hard, and trying to show that I wasn't totally disorientated by what had just transpired.

"What if another noise spike showed in that trace, and we switched off the experiment immediately?"

"Then you'd be grandfathering," Margaret said. "Sending a causal change upstream, which in turn affects the downstream reality. A true paradox, albeit a relatively mild one. But I can easily demonstrate a low-level paradox without turning off the experiment." Her eyes flicked to a wall clock, a digital counter in a black surround. "In sixty seconds I'll drop this pen again."

I returned my gaze to the noise trace. Immediately a similar spike appeared, and after a few seconds the brackets and statistical parameters appeared.

"All right . . ." I said, eyeing Margaret carefully.

Margaret walked softly to another bench and picked

up a second pen. Now she held them both, one in each hand. "You see one spike at the moment, agreed?"

"Agreed."

"That's because our downstream reality reflects an upstream case in which I dropped only one pen, as I promised. That's a closed loop, paradox-free. But I'm going to violate it, by dropping two pens."

The single spike was drifting to the left, now about thirty seconds downstream of our present position. I thought about what would happen when we caught up with the future moment in which Margaret had dropped only one pen. Now there would be two acoustic events, and the Luba Pairs would respond accordingly. The digital trace would have to show two noise spikes, instead of the one that was still visible.

But it hadn't.

Something will happen, I thought, to preserve the present condition. Margaret would drop one pen and it would hit the floor just like the one I'd dropped. But the second would hit her shoe, muffling its impact, so that there was still only one acoustic event. Even that would be weird. But there'd be no paradox, no grandfathering.

The digital clock showed sixty seconds since Margaret picked up the first pen. She dropped it, waited a second, then dropped the second. Both pens had hit the floor, as loudly as the first time.

"We've modified the upstream condition," Margaret said. "The past will now adjust itself to reflect this. But it doesn't happen instantly. We call it causal-lag, a sort of inertia or stickiness."

"It's an outgrowth of your mother's work," Antti put in.

"We're now in a superposition of histories," Margaret continued. "There's the fading state, in which there was just one noise event, and the rising state, in which there are two events. Gradually the rising state will supplant the fading one. Our minds are easily capable of perceiving both histories, until the new condition becomes dominant."

My attention returned to the noise readout. The original spike was still there, but a fresh prominence was rising out of the noise to its right, like a second peak thrusting up from a mountain range. This new spike quickly became as significant as the first, bracketed and annotated. These were noise events that had already been recorded on the system ninety seconds ago.

I blinked.

There was a fuzziness to my thoughts, like the first pleasant stages of drunkenness.

I remembered that there had been one spike. I also remembered that there had *always been two*. My brain was holding two histories within itself, and it was no different, no stranger, no more paradoxical, than crossing my eyes and seeing two slightly offset versions of the same scene.

Antti and Margaret regarded me with a quiet, knowing watchfulness. They'd been through this already, numerous times. It wasn't unusual to them at all.

I thought of the causal-lag Margaret had mentioned.

I remembered my mother at her whiteboard, a summer or two before that bust-up, rubbing out and rehashing one idea after the next. Trying to break through to a new model of time, a fresh way of thinking about the relationships between past and future events, the illusion of the ever-moving now. Time wasn't a river, she said, and it wasn't a circuit-diagram. Nor was it a tree with multiple branches. It was a block structure, more like a crystal lattice than any of those old dead-end paradigms. It was a lattice that spanned the entire existence of the universe, from beginning to end. There were no alternate histories, no branches where the Roman empire never fell or the dinosaurs were never wiped out. Just that single lattice, a single fixed structure. We were in it, embedded in its matrix.

But the lattice wasn't static. There were flaws in it—imperfections, impurities and stress points. What the lattice was trying to do was to settle down into a minimum-energy configuration. But in doing so, those stresses could give way suddenly or propagate a long way from their initial positions. That was the lattice adjusting itself, history settling into a new, temporary configuration. The alterations happened naturally, time murmuring to itself like an old house, but they could also be generated by artificial interventions, such as Margaret's paradox with the two pens. Then, a pattern of changes would ripple through the lattice, the future changing the past, the past changing the future, the future returning the favour, like a series of dying echoes, until a new configuration held sway. But that adjustment process wasn't instantaneous from the point of view of an embedded observer. It was more like the thunderclap arriving after a lighting flash, a delayed portent of the same event. Causal-lag.

But what paradox, exactly?

There'd always been two spikes. Margaret had said she would drop two pens, and the system had detected her future intention, and she had followed through one minute later.

No. I almost had to frown to hold onto it. There'd been that other condition. One spike, not two. One pen drop. It was slipping away, though—hard to recollect, hard to think about. Like a dream fragment that shrivelled to nothing in the light of day.

Gape-mouthed, I stared at my new colleagues.

"What just happened?"

"What do you remember?" Margaret asked.

"Almost nothing. Just that . . ." But I could only shake my own head. "It's gone. Whatever it was, it's gone."

"Do you feel normal?" Antti asked.

"No. Not normal." I steadied myself on the bench. My cane was outside, waiting for me to collect it. "Yes. Normal. But there was something. There *was* something. I just can't hold onto it now."

"We grandfathered," Margaret said. "That's all it could have been. You must have asked us to demonstrate a paradox condition, and we set one up. Swapped one future for another, and then the past swapped around to keep track." She grinned, stooping down to collect the two fallen pens. "It's strange, isn't it?"

I let out a breath. "Crap!"

"Generally the first reaction," Antti said, with a faint approving smile, as if I'd crossed some unspoken threshold of acceptance. "Gets easier, though. Less strange. These are only small paradoxes, after all. You just buckle up and ride the turbulence. Be glad we never go near anything big."

I'd regained enough composure to pay attention to what she was saying. "And if we did?"

"Oh, we can't—luckily," Margaret said. "The noise swamps us long before we ever get close to doing anything *really* stupid."

---

So I was inducted into the work of Permafrost, a step at a time.

But why that name, exactly, for Director Cho's experiment?

Throughout my time at the station he had never explained it. Appropriate enough for a place so cold, so remote, I supposed. Yet there was also a sense of stillness, changelessness, which must have been an allusion to my mother's block-crystal model of time.

Time as a solid, glacial structure, groaning to itself as defects propagated through its frozen matrix, yet essentially fixed, immutable, persistent, enduring. Time as a white thing, a white landscape, under white skies and ominous squared-off clouds.

Time as a self-reinforcing structure in which all memory of humanity had been quietly erased.

---

The doctor and the orderly wheeled me to radiology.

*You think I'm going to let you stab someone with that knife?*

*That's not the idea. And even if it was, you wouldn't be able to do much about it, so just sit back and let me handle things.*

My arm, the one that was concealing the knife, twitched in my lap. It was a moment of spasm, no more than that, but it was nothing I'd initiated.

*You saw that, didn't you?*

*Be careful.*

*Or what? I'll drop the knife, and then what'll happen?*

*What'll happen is that we'll both be in trouble, Tatiana. That machine ahead of us is going to kill you if you get anywhere near it. The knife is how we're going to take the machine out of service, before it turns your brain into hot mush.*

*I'm so glad that you're concerned.*

*I am. You're the only body I get to control. I have a duty to make sure you don't end up dead.*

*So very considerate.*

*Believe it or not, I also don't want you to get hurt in any part of this. You're an innocent party here. I appreciate that you're angry, but you also have to understand that we're acting for a greater good.*

*Such a great good, you can't trust me with knowing any part of it. How's that for trust?*

*Shut up and let me handle this.*

The big red doors hissed open on their own as we came near. Beyond was a brighter area, a sort of reception and waiting room with short windowless corridors branching off to the different functions of the department. The MRI section was at the end of one of these corridors, behind another set of red doors.

The space beyond was subdivided into two equal areas, with a glass partition between them. In the first part was the control room for the scanner, with a long desk set with terminals and keyboards. In the other was the scanner itself, with that area kept scrupulously clear of any furniture or associated clutter. The control room was low-lit and spartan, with a technician seated at one of the monitors, clicking away on a computer mouse, taking the occasional sip from a plastic coffee cup.

"Good morning," the young doctor said.

The technician swivelled around and touched a deferential hand to his brow. "Good morning, Dr. Turovsky. Good morning, Igor." Then he nodded at me, and flicked an eye back to his screens. "Miss Dinova."

"Is it working today?" I asked.

"We'll be fine; it was just a stupid software problem." The technician was a burly man in his thirties, with a black chinbeard and tattoos showing around his sleeves and neckline. "They made us install a new operating system—you know how that usually goes."

*It's an MRI machine, Valentina. I've already been through it, and it didn't kill me. What's changed now?*

*You have.*

*Enigmatic to the end. Are you all like that, where you come from? Kogalym, wasn't it? Or some other Siberian shithole?*

*I'm telling you exactly as much as I think you need, exactly as much as I think you can handle. No more. But you're right about the MRI machine. It didn't kill you before, but that's because we weren't inside you then. The postoperative scan? That's when we dropped something into you. That little spore I mentioned, a pollen-sized speck of replicating machinery, containing one half of a quantum particle system called a Luba Pair. Delivered straight into your neocortex. Military-medical hardware, primed to grow into a living brain and establish sensorimotor dominance. Think of it as a kind of ghostly lace overlaying your own brain, mirroring a similar structure in my own head. We need the MRI machine to get it into you, like a kind of long-range syringe, but once it's installed and growing, the link maintains itself. That's what's in you now, how we're able to communicate, how I get to drive you.*

*Drive me. That's a nice way of putting it.*

*Only saying it as it is. No point sparing anyone's feelings here, is there?*

*And they used to tell me I was blunt.*

*Face it, Tatiana—we're probably not so very different. You're caught up in me, and I'm caught up in something else. Both being used. Both dealing with something big and frightening outside our usual experience. And yes, you were right about Kogalym.*

"May I see the earlier images?" the young doctor said, leaning in to the desk.

"I pulled them up for you," the technician said. "Before—after. You can see that cloudiness."

"Looks more like an imaging issue, something off with the resolution?"

*What's he looking at?*

*The control structure, before it was fully grown and integrated. Developed enough to show up on the MRI, but not enough to be seriously affected by the magnetic fields. It'll be different now, trust me.*

*Trust you?*

*You'd better. We're both in this now.*

The technician gave an equivocal shrug. "Only one way to be sure, Doctor, if you think it's worth the expense of a second scan."

"I want to be sure for Miss Dinova's sake," said the doctor.

"Let's get you out of the chair," the orderly—Igor—said.

But I was ahead of him, pushing myself up and out of the wheelchair. What I did next was all choreographed, but it had to look natural. Just as importantly, Tatiana had to let me handle things.

She did.

I made an intentional step in the direction of the desk, meaning to get a closer look at the brain scans. Halfway there, I let my left knee buckle under me. I followed through with the stumble, allowing momentum to carry me forward, while reaching for the desk's edge, misjudging it such that I knocked the coffee cup over.

All this happened in about one and a half seconds.

"I'm sorry," I muttered. "I didn't mean . . ."

The technician pushed back his swivel chair, lifting up his arms in despair as coffee—what had not gone into the keyboard—curtained off the side of the desk in brown rivulets. Igor, who was evidently more practically minded, dashed forward and flipped the keyboard upside down, to stop the liquid getting any farther into its workings. But the essential damage had been done. The screens flickered then froze, none of the displays updating.

*Exactly what was that about?*

*I saw a moment, went for it.*

"That's done it!" the technician said, shaking his head in annoyance and disbelief at my incredible clumsiness.

"I've had brain surgery," I said, as Igor shoved me back into the wheelchair. "Give me a break, won't you?"

*You're right—you've just had brain surgery. You shouldn't be taking any nonsense from anyone. All right, I'm almost impressed.*

*Thank you . . .*

The technician rolled his chair to the left, where he was attempting to reboot the monitors with the second keyboard, hammering repeatedly at the same keys.

"It's no good—she's really screwed it up." He began to reach for the desk telephone. "Someone's going to have to come in and sort this out, and you know how long that usually takes."

The knife slid from my sleeve.

It was a while since I'd had a chance to press the bracelet back up my forearm. The knife landed on my knee and just for an instant there was every chance it was going to remain there, before it slid off and clattered to the floor.

*That wasn't me. I didn't do that.*

*I know.*

"A knife!" Igor called, dragging back the wheelchair, with me in it. "She had a knife on her!"

The technician stared at me with doubt and bewilderment. Presumably I had been the model patient on my previous visits to the radiology department, and yet now I was this destructive, knife-concealing lunatic.

"I don't know how that knife ended up on me," I said.

Igor leaned over the back of the wheelchair, pushing down on my shoulders. "It was up her sleeve. I saw it come out."

The technician rolled his seat the limit of the desk, where it met the wall. "Damn it, I've had enough of this."

He thumped his fist against a red call button and an alarm began to sound.

*You got a plan for this, Valentina?*

I forced myself out of the chair, using all my strength to ram it back into Igor. Igor grunted and tried to wrestle me back into the seat. Now that my elbow was free I jabbed him hard in the ribs and twisted away from him. Perhaps if he'd been a law enforcement official or guard he'd have been better equipped to stop me, but Igor was just an orderly and I think my burst of strength and action was more than he was prepared for. The young doctor had the knife now, but he was holding it up and away from me, while Igor rolled the chair in front of the hallway door, as if he meant to use it as a barricade.

The alarm continued sounding.

"You're confused," the young doctor said, extending his right hand in a calming gesture. "And frightened. But there's no need to be. You can't be held accountable for behaviour that's completely out of character. This is just some postoperative confusion that we should have . . ."

With the technician at the far end of the desk, Igor at the door, and the young doctor preoccupied with the knife, I saw my opportunity. It was on the desk, between the monitors, under a flip-up plastic lid. A fat green emergency button, the kind you could hammer down with a fist.

I sprang for it. The technician made to block me, but he wasn't nearly fast enough.

A grey fog hit.

———————

The shock of the transition was so sudden that I nearly jerked out of the padding, a sleeper rudely awoken.

I drew a breath, fighting for control and composure. Cho and his technicians were present, looking on with concern.

"Why'd you bring me out?"

"We didn't!" Cho said defensively. "You were noise-swamped. It happened very quickly, over the course of about twenty seconds. What was happening?"

The memory of Tatiana's body was still with me. I could feel the bandage around her head, the soreness in her rib cage where I had banged the desk. Igor's hands on my shoulders, the knife in the crook of my elbow.

"Get me back in," I said. "Fight the noise."

"You're grandfathering," Cho said, while Margaret and the other technicians fussed at their machines. "Hitting paradox limits. Be clear. What was happening? Were you anywhere near the MRI machine?"

I wanted to be back in the room, back in Tatiana. She was more than just some anonymous host now. We'd spoken to each other, established . . . something. Not exactly trust, but a step on the way to it. And I'd bailed out of her, leaving her to deal with the mess I'd initiated.

"I was trying to shut it down," I said. "Going for the

quench button."

"That was the absolute last resort," Cho answered, with a rising strain.

"I'd tried everything else. I thought I'd disabled the machine at the software interface, but then things went wrong. I had a knife on me, and it slipped out. They called security, and they were on their way." I twisted my neck, addressing the nearest of the technicians. "Get me back in."

"We're trying different noise filters," Margaret said. "You're still close to the threshold. The neural traffic was going stochastic even before you came back. Was anything off about the immersion?"

I hesitated, on the brink of telling her everything. How Tatiana was in my head, and I was in Tatiana's. How she'd managed to override my motor control for a moment, twitching her arm. How she'd reported a glimpse of this room, visual data feeding back the wrong way, into the past instead of up to the future. She'd seen the *Vaymyr*, seen the inside of an icebreaker fifty-two years upstream.

But a glitch at this stage could be all the excuse Cho needed for pulling me off the team. The pressure was on him, this man who had already given so much. It had been controversial, moving me up after the problem with Christos. Cho's only justification had been that I was technically competent, had a good understanding of the protocol, and already had a neural system that could be adapted to work with the Permafrost technology.

There was some justifiable resentment. No one blamed me for Christos, but I knew there was irritation that, of all of us, I had been the one who jumped the queue, the one who ended up going back in time before the others—even though there'd been no predicting which of us would be the first.

Still, faced with a complication, Cho might decide to abandon Tatiana. I couldn't abandon her like that.

"It was all right," I said. "But I have to get back."

Cho rubbed at his forehead. "This is very bad. If you were committed to a course of action then you may have completed it, even in the absence of a fully functioning link. A helium quench is a very serious business."

Cho vanished: so did the technicians and the rest of the room.

Just a flash came through, similar in duration to that first glimpse of Tatiana's timeline. The room looked odd. The desk was at right angles, going up toward the ceiling. The swivel chair was sticking out sideways. The technician was slumped over on the desk, just as impossibly. A geometric surface stretched away from me, with a moundlike form not far off. Everything was slightly out of focus, tonally diffuse. I concentrated, trying to mesh my perceptions with Tatiana's viewpoint. She was on the floor, and the moundlike form was someone else lying near me.

*Tatiana?*

No answer.

I moved. A crawl was the best I could do. It was like fighting through thickening fluid, each action harder than the one that had preceded it. It must have taken ten or twelve seconds just to inch my way to the door, and then I had to reach high enough to tug down on the handle, using my weight to attempt to swing the door inward. It didn't want to open against the helium pressure in the room. My vision was starting to darken. I put all my force into the door. I only had to open it a crack, and the helium would flood out and equalise the pressure on either side.

The door gave. I crawled through the widening gap, half in and half out of the MRI room, and then I was done. I had exhausted the last reserves of energy from Tatiana's body; she could give no more. As my vision faded to tunnel darkness I had just a glimpse of figures approaching along the hallway, moving with the crouched caution of men and women not sure what they are getting themselves into.

The last thing I sensed was some stiff, masklike thing being pressed against my face.

———————

Dr. Abramik gave me a brief but thorough physical before agreeing to send me in again. There was no possibility of anything that had happened to Tatiana affecting me physically, but I'd still spent many hours in the dental chair, and with that enforced immobility came a risk of pressure sores and deep vein thrombosis. I had the kind of deep, lingering stiffness that only came after sleeping in an awkward position. After I'd walked around on the deck of the *Vaymyr* for a quarter of an hour, though, flapping my arms and stomping my feet, and taken in some of the cold but invigorating air, I felt I could cope with going back in again.

I wanted to, as well. I'd made something bad happen in the MRI theatre and I felt I owed it to myself, as well as those who'd been caught up in the helium quench, to understand the consequences. That meant going back into Tatiana's world.

Had I done any real harm? It was hard to say.

She'd had follow-up appointments stretching between early July and early August, and there was a note about a civil case involving criminal damage to hospital property—occurring in the same time frame—being dropped due to expert medical opinion holding that she couldn't be held accountable for her actions.

I squinted, slightly puzzled that I'd missed that detail the first time around. Or had I? Perhaps I *had* read it, but had been focussing more on the medical history.

No; that was definitely what had happened.

It all made sense, at least. Cho had even showed me the service record of time-probe eighteen, which was recorded on a metal plate near the base of the chassis. In June 2028, engineers from the manufacturer had carried out an otherwise routine helium recharge and recalibration, proving that no lasting harm had been done by the quench operation. Tatiana would have had her follow-up appointments sooner after discharge, but she'd had to wait for the machine to be put back into service.

I dealt with the strangeness of that. I felt that I'd caused the helium quench, but according to Cho it was already baked into the history of the time-probe.

"I have examined that service plate many times," he said. "And you have my categorical assurance that there has been no change."

My head was hurting with all this. "Then why were we so concerned that I'd screw things up by triggering the quench?"

Cho looked at me with a frown of his own, as if I was the one making headaches. "No—our concern was completely the opposite; that your interventions would somehow delay or impede the quench that we knew was obliged to happen."

I nodded slowly, feeling as if the gentle force of his words, so calmly uttered, was pushing me into an acceptance of one version of the facts over another. For a moment I clung onto a different narrative, one in which the helium quench had been viewed as a very damaging act, something to be avoided except as a last resort, but already I could feel that version becoming thinner, less persuasive, a counterfactual daydream that no longer had the conviction of reality.

No: Cho was right. The problem had always been how to guarantee that the quench occurred. Preventing or delaying it could have caused all sorts of dangerous upstream ramifications.

At least now we were still on track.

The other pilots were gathered around the dental chair. I could sense their emotions, the mixture of frustration, jealousy and comradely concern. It rankled them that I'd been the first to go into time. But I was also one of them now, and they had protective feelings toward me.

"She needs a longer rest than this," Antti said, directing her remark at Cho. "It's not good to send her in so soon after the last immersion. She hasn't eaten or slept!"

"I'm all right," I said, smiling back my reassurance. "I rested in the hospital, and I'm not really hungry."

"She's getting mixed signals from the host," Vikram

said. "Thinking she's rested, thinking she's had a decent meal."

"I know what I can take," I insisted.

"I am willing to let her go back," Dr. Abramik said. "But if this immersion lasts as long as the one before, I'll insist on a twenty-four-hour rest interval afterward."

"I am in complete agreement," Cho replied. "Our pilots are a precious resource, and we must treat them well. Equally, we must obtain data on the downstream situation. The Brothers confirm that they are still reading neuro-telemetry from the host. That means that whatever happened in the MRI theatre, Tatiana Dinova is still alive, still receptive. Are you prepared, Miss Lidova?"

"I'm ready," I said.

"The link is now reinstated," Margaret said. "You should immerse almost . . ."

Immediately.

Lights were strobing. I was looking up at a pale surface, which was being periodically lit and unlit by a blue-white light. I stared at it for a few moments, gathering my orientation. Something hard was pinching my face, and a woman in a uniform was leaning over me, steadying herself against an overhead rack full of medical devices.

Movement under me. The rumble of wheels and a motor. The blue-white lights were streetlamps, whisking by outside.

The woman loosened my mask so I could talk, then held up her hand.

"Good—you're awake. How many fingers?"

"Five," I said, trying to sound groggy but present. "Four and a thumb."

"That's excellent. And can you tell me your name?"

"Tatiana," I answered sluggishly, and not merely because I was putting on an act, but because I also had to make an effort to keep our two names separated in my head. Of all the people I could have jumped into, why had fate given me a woman with a name whose rhythm and sounds were so close to my own? "Tatiana Dinova."

*Welcome back, Valentina whatever-the-hell-you're-called. My head feels like someone opened it with an axe. I suppose you know what happened back there?*

*I broke the MRI machine. Released all the helium inside it. Something went wrong, though, and the helium built up inside the control room. You were unconscious. I was inside you, and nobody else was home. I crawled you out, and some paramedics came. Now we're in an ambulance.*

*Going where?*

*I have no idea.*

"Tatiana? Are you still there?"

*You'd better answer the lady. She might start thinking one of us has brain damage.*

"I'm here."

"And where are we now, Tatiana?"

"I don't know. You're driving me somewhere."

"What's the last thing you remember?"

"Radiology. The MRI theatre. Then something…" I shook my head, aware that there was something squatting in it like a heavy black thundercloud. Tatiana must have had a monstrous headache after being unconscious. I was getting the ragged edges of it, not the thing itself, but it was enough to earn my sympathy. "I don't know. I don't remember anything after getting there."

"There was a screwup. By the time we got there four of you were on the floor, already suffocating."

"Why am I in an ambulance, if I'm already in a hospital?"

*Now that is a very good question. I couldn't have put it better myself.*

"Because it's a big mess in that whole wing. Everything's locked down while they vent the helium. Can't get a crash cart through, and even if we could, it's still quicker to drive you around the perimeter road to emergency admissions, just as if you'd had an accident outside the hospital. Anyway, it looks as if we got you onto oxygen in good time. You probably don't feel all that great, but you're giving me clear, coherent answers, and that's what I want to hear."

*Tell her my head feels like an axe split it open.*

"What about the others... the young doctor?" I fought to recall his name, the name I'd heard the MRI technician mention. "Dr. Turovsky, and Igor. The man in the theatre."

"They'll be getting all the care they need. Worry about yourself for now. You're the patient, the one who's been messed around by this accident."

I felt an empathic connection with this woman, moved by her kindness and devotion to public care. I didn't know the first thing about her, not her name, not her time of birth or death, what had happened to her in the difficulties, what sort of life she'd led, but in that moment I knew that she was a good and decent person, that the past was full of people like her, that it was just as valid to think of history being stitched together out of numerous tiny acts of selflessness and consideration, as it was to view it as a grand, sweeping spectacle of vast impersonal triumphs and tragedies.

"Thank you," I mouthed.

*From both of us.*

We tipped over.

There was a side impact, the ambulance tilted, then flipped onto its side. The ambulance woman slammed into the shelf, slumping into instant unconsciousness. I would have been thrown hard against the sidewall, except that I'd already been strapped onto a stretcher.

Even then, the impact was bruising. Motionless now, the ambulance spun its wheels, the motor still revving. The ambulance woman was lying over me, a gash in her forehead, out cold. I hoped she was out cold, at least.

I tried moving. I was thinking that there had to be a driver in the front compartment, someone else who might be hurt. I hadn't caused whatever had just happened to us, but I was responsible for this ambulance being here in the first place. I struggled against my restraints. With the ambulance woman pressed over me, it was too hard to reach the straps.

*Was this part of your big, carefully thought-out plan, Valentina?*

*No. Not at all.*

*That's good to know. I'd hate to feel I wasn't in capable hands.*

Someone opened the rear doors, shining a light into the interior. The torch beam settled on my face, lingering there for a second. The person climbed into the ambulance, grunting as they pushed against what was now the upper door, holding it open against the force of gravity. It was a man, middle-aged, quite burly and thickset, and not wearing any sort of hospital or civil uniform, just a scruffy leather jacket over a thick sweater. The man clambered in, setting down the torch, and moved the ambulance woman off me.

"Did you just drive into us?" I asked.

The man eased the ambulance woman down onto what had been the sidewall, but which was now the floor. Then he undid my straps and began to move me off the stretcher, none too gently. "Get out. Police are on their way. We need to drive."

*Do you know this man?*

*No. Not at all.*

*Then can I suggest you ask him who the hell he is?*

I did just that.

The man looked at me with a combination of contempt and amusement. He had a face full of stubble, a heavily veined nose, bags under his eyes and a shock of thick black hair bristling up from a very low hairline, almost meeting his eyebrows.

"Who am I?" he said. "Oh, that's easy. We've already met. I'm Antti."

---

He had a car waiting. It was not the same car he had used to sideswipe the ambulance, which was now badly damaged around the front wheel. He'd planned it, I thought. Planned to ram the ambulance, and known he'd need a second vehicle, which he had parked on the perimeter road, ready for us.

*So let's clear this up. You don't know this man, but you do know him?*

*I know Antti. Antti's someone else, another member of the team. A pilot, like me. Except . . .*

He helped me into the passenger seat, then went round to the driver's side. He got in, started the car, flooring the throttle hard, swerving onto the road and sending us barrelling away from the scene of the crash. I tilted my head, catching my reflection in the side mirror. It was the first time I'd seen Tatiana Dinova properly. It was an exceedingly strange thing, to look in a mirror and see a difference face staring back. There was a whole system of brain circuitry being confused, a system that had spent a lifetime being lulled into the idea that it had an adequate understanding of reality.

*Anyone tell you it's rude to stare?*

*I'm sorry.*

I looked through her. Beyond the face, beyond the too-thin bone structure, the eyes that were the wrong shape and colour, the nose that didn't belong, the bandage, the pressure marks from the oxygen mask.

Beyond to several pairs of moving flashing lights, as other emergency vehicles came nearer.

"You can't be Antti," I said, once we'd turned off the perimeter road, onto a connecting road that took us away from the main hospital complex.

*The billion-rouble question!*

The thickset man took his eyes off the wheel long enough to glance at me. "And why's that, exactly?"

"Because I'm the first. No one else has gone into time yet. There's just four pilots: you, me, Vikram and Miguel, and no one else has done it yet." I smacked the console in front of me. "Crap, I was just talking to you, Antti! About two minutes ago. You were trying to tell Cho that I needed a rest, that I was being sent in again too soon."

*So, let's get this straight—for my benefit, if no one else's. You've been sent back from the future, and you thought you were the only one who'd done it so far. But now this guy shows up, and he's acting as if he's already ahead of you?*

The man spun the wheel hard, negotiating a mini roundabout. The flashing blue lights were farther away now. Ahead was a complex of industrial-looking buildings, warehouses and factory units. I wasn't even sure that we were still within the hospital grounds.

"I remember that conversation," the man said. "The only difference is it was about nine months ago."

"What the fuck!"

*What the fuck, indeed! I like your style, Val. Do all school-teachers swear like you in the future?*

"You were right," he answered, calmly enough. "You were the first of us to go into time. Didn't seem fair, to begin with, you skipping ahead like that. But Margaret always said there was an element of uncertainty about which of us would get the first immersion, depending on how quickly the control structures meshed. Get down."

"What?"

*You heard the man.*

He pushed me hard, forcing me to squeeze down low in the passenger seat. He slowed, raised his hand in a greeting, and I caught the top of a police van, passing us on the left.

He drove on straight for a little while, flicking his eyes to the rearview mirror, then turned onto another road.

"I don't think they saw you. Any other police cars or ambulances, you duck down, all right? At least until we're a long way out of Izhevsk. They'll be looking for a patient who matches your description, and I don't want to take any chances."

"All right—from the start. What. Is. Happening." I was calmer now, if still bewildered. "I accept that you're Antti. You've told me too much for that not to be the case. And this was all deliberate, wasn't it? Hitting that ambulance, being ready to drive me away?"

"I had time to prepare." He tightened his hands on the wheel, picking up speed as we exited the industrial area and moved onto a divided carriageway. "Eight months. That's how long it's been, how long I've been time-embedded. You understand now, right? You were the first to go into the time. I came after. But I went deeper—leapfrogged over you. The time-probe sent me back eight months earlier than you."

"No!"

"Is that, no, as in you don't believe me, or no, as in you never considered this possibility?"

*Give the man credit, this has got to be messing with his head as well as yours and mine.*

I was silent for a few moments. That thundercloud was still hovering in my skull, and all the swerving and hard cornering was making me nauseous. "Then you know what happens to me. You said that conversation was nine months old, and you've been embedded for eight. That means you know how this plays out for at least another month, maybe more."

"To a degree."

"What does that mean?"

"It means that we're swimming in some deep paradox here, Valentina. Black, grey, all the shades your mother painted. I know it, Cho knows it, Margaret Arbetsumian knew it."

"What do you mean, Margaret *knew* it?"

"Margaret's dead. Upstream Margaret. She couldn't take it anymore. She realised what we've done ... what we're doing. It's all falling to pieces, the whole experiment. We opened up something we don't understand, a whole box of snakes."

*You knew this Margaret?*

*Yes. Knew her and liked her. But she was alive the last time I saw her and she'll be alive when I go back. You probably saw her as well. The people, the machines, that room with no windows? She'd have been there, watching.*

*Small, glasses, straight fringe?*

*Yes. Margaret.*

*She didn't look very dead to me.*

*She wouldn't have been, not then, not yet.*

*I'm . . . sorry. Hell, why am I the one apologising? You're in my head without permission, and I'm feeling sorry for you because someone died, someone else involved in this shit?*

*Because you're the same as me, Tatiana. Not a bad person, just caught up in something bigger than you. And it's Lidova. Valentina Lidova, as in Luba Lidova. Just as long as we're getting to know each other.*

The car accelerated again. "We've got a safe house," Antti said, "about a hundred kilometres out of Izhevsk. There's some stuff we need to discuss. Oh, and you'll get to meet Vikram again."

"Vikram's come back as well?"

Antti said nothing.

———

Rain was falling by the time we made it to the safe house, about an hour's drive out of Izhevsk. The light was dusky, the bellies of the clouds shaded with purple. It was still only midday: everything that had happened since I was wheeled to the MRI theatre had been squeezed into no more than six hours, including the helium event, the ambulance smash and being driven away by Antti.

We kept on the main highway for about thirty minutes, then pulled off onto smaller roads. Eventually we passed through a wooded area and I asked Antti to pull over so I could go behind some trees and puke.

I retched and retched until I was dry heaving.

*Nicely done, Val. Better out than in.*

*Glad you appreciate the gesture. Have you any idea where we are?*

*Why should I?*

*Because you're from Izhevsk.*

*I am. That doesn't mean I memorised every shitty back road within a hundred kilometres of the place.*

I didn't feel much better getting back into the car, but my head was sharper, my thoughts more organised.

"I believe everything you've told me," I said eventually, when we were moving again. "But you weren't meant to be injected into a man. What the hell went wrong?"

His jaw moved before answering, some calculation

working behind his eyes. His eyes/her eyes. I knew there was a woman behind them, but it was a man I was looking at, a man talking to me, and now I couldn't help but see Antti as a male presence, a hard man with drinker's features and worker's hands, someone who moved with an easy assumption of authority.

"We were running out of options. The noise was rising. Sending you back in, putting you into Tatiana Dinova, caused some upset."

*No arguing with that. At least one of you has some basic human empathy.*

*He means a different kind of upset.*

*I gathered.*

"It was getting harder for the time-probes to get a positive lock," Antti went on. "Even when we managed to inject, the telemetry was much too noisy to be sure who we were in. We couldn't analyse the biochemical environment properly, couldn't get a clear phenotypic signature. With you, Cho knew you were going to mesh with a female host subject. With me, it was more a question of taking our chances." He paused. "I'm all right. I got used to this body pretty quickly. It works for me."

"Who are you? Downstream, I mean."

"Tibor's my host."

"And this . . . Tibor. Have you had any . . . contact . . . ?"

He looked at me carefully, only part of his attention on

the road ahead. "Meaning what?"

I decided I'd wait to tell Antti about Tatiana, assuming I told him at all. It was time to hear his side of things, first. Then I'd decide what he needed to know.

———————

The property was a farmhouse, safely distant from any other buildings or prying eyes. It was reached down a long, rutted, dirt track. As a base for conducting our embedded time-operations, it was virtually perfect, even if a little run-down, damp and chilly, even in June. Antti parked the car in an enclosing courtyard, next to another mud-splattered car and a semiderelict tractor, and then took me into the main building and through to a kitchen. There was electricity. He sat me down at a wooden table, asked if I was feeling all right after the drive, evincing something close to tenderness for the first time since our encounter.

"It's a jolt, I know." He set about boiling some water. "At least I was semiprepared. Once we had a lock, we thought it was likely to take me deeper than you, and there was only a fifty-fifty chance I got injected into a female host."

"What did Vikram get?" I asked, wondering why we hadn't yet been reintroduced.

"Do you want tea or coffee?"

*Tea. Two sugars. Some honey if you can stretch to it.*

I nodded at the jar next to his hand. "Coffee. Strong. How did you find this place?"

"My host's brother owns it. The brother's on an oil contract in Kazakhstan, and he left the keys with Tibor, along with a lot of other useful stuff like access to his bank account. Trusting brother! It'll do while we're here, which won't be long now."

"You say there's still a chance to put things right."

With his back to me, Antti spooned coffee into a waiting cup.

"Under the table."

I groped around until I found whatever he was on about. It was a handle, connected to a bulky alloy case with angled corners and a digital readout next to the lock.

I hefted the case onto the table, pushing aside a telephone book to make room, and waiting for Antti to offer further elucidation. I didn't dare open it. The lock looked like the kind of thing that might trigger a built-in bomb or set off nerve gas.

"What is it?"

"Cho's seeds," Antti said while he poured in the boiling water.

I was surprised, elated, then instantly doubtful.

"Are you sure? It can't have been that easy."

"What was easy about it? I told you I've been time-embedded for eight months." He came back with two cups of coffee, and lowered himself into the seat opposite mine. The wooden chair creaked under his frame. He had rolled up the sleeves of his sweater, revealing hairy arms heavily corded with muscle, bruised by old, fading tattoos. "It's taken most of that time to acquire the seeds. There's a privately operated seed vault just over the Finnish border, a very long drive from here. It took three goes to get close to it, two to get inside. Fortunately the security wasn't that stringent, I could easily pass myself off as a local contractor, and no one involved had any real idea of the value of these seeds. Why would they? Just another genetically modified test sample, a commercial dead-end." Some dark amusement played behind his eyes. "They've no idea of the trouble that's coming."

"May I open them?"

"You can open the outer layer. There's no need to go farther than that."

"Code?"

"Two, zero, eight, zero."

I entered the digital combination. The case clicked, and the lid opened slightly. I pushed it back the rest of the way. Inside was a second case, presumably to allow for additional protection of the contents. This one was white, with its own digital security system, and an armoured window offering a view of the contents. It was fixed to the outer case, so there was no way the two could be separated.

I scuffed my sleeve across the fogged window. Under it was a padded container with stoppered glass capsules packed into slots, each capsule labelled with a bar code and containing what looked like a few thimblefuls of dirt.

"These are the real deal?"

"They'll do."

"Then ... it's done. We've got what we came for." I tried to read his/her face, wondering why he was holding back from any sort of celebration. "Help me out here, Antti. What's the difficulty?"

*Help me out as well. Why are we getting so excited about a case full of dirt?*

*They're seeds. Genetically modified seeds. Windblown propagators. Really hardy—you could almost grow them on Mars, if you had to. Practically valueless now, but incredibly important fifty-two years in the future.*

*Why?*

*Something bad happens around 2050. At first, we almost don't notice it. There's a steepening in the rate at which insect species are going extinct, but even then it just seems to be part of a pattern of something that's been going on for a long time, and to begin with only a few scientists are really worried. But it gets worse, and really quickly. No one really understands what's happening. There's talk of horizontal gene-transfer, of some rogue mutation, perhaps some deliberate thing, a biological weapon gone haywire, hopping from one insect species to the next. Shutting them down, like a computer virus. Within five years, almost all insect life is gone. But it doesn't end there. Plant pollination stops, of course, and then animals higher up the food chain start suffering. Insectivores die off pretty quickly, birds and small mammals, and then the rest, everything that depends on them. Meanwhile, the gene-transfer or whatever it was doesn't stop happening. Insects first, then marine invertebrates—and once they go, all the oceans shut down. Humans manage, for a while. We had a lot of systems in place to buffer us from the immediate effects. But it's only a temporary lull, before it starts hurting us as well. Crops fail. Soils start to turn sterile. Decomposition processes falter, triggering a second public health emergency beyond the initial famine. Within a decade, the effects are global and climatic. Dust storms, aridification, mass migration. A gradual collapse of social order. We had to give a name to the whole thing so we called it the Scouring: an environmental and biological cascade. Not much comes through the other side; certainly not enough for anyone to live on. All animal and plant life gone, except for a few laboratory specimens. By 2080, we're down to stored rations, the last human generation.*

She absorbed my words. They had flowed easily enough. As a teacher, even a mathematics teacher, I had been called on often enough to explain our current predicament, and how it had come about.

*Well, I can't wait to live through that.*

*You don't . . .*

But I caught myself.

*What? What were you about to say?*

"Don't you see?" Antti ladled sugar into his coffee, more than I remembered *her* ever taking, when we were in the canteen. "This is only half the job, Valentina. We've got the seeds, yes. Now we've got to get them back to Cho, somehow—fifty-two years in the future. That's the hard part. These seeds have still got to take the long way around." Then he angled his head and spoke into the room adjoining the kitchen. "Vikram! Wake up. I'm with Valentina. Come and say hello."

*What were you about to tell me? That I don't get to see the trouble that's coming? That I'm already dead, twenty years from now? Was that it?*

I tilted my head toward the doorway. "Is something wrong with Vikram?"

"Dying," Antti said, with a surprising coldness. "Not long to go now."

Nobody came into the kitchen immediately, and there

was no sound of movement or footsteps from anywhere nearby, so I returned my thoughts to the seed samples.

"We had a plan. Still *have* a plan. The seeds need to be relocated, taken to a different seed vault—one we know will come through the difficulties. Cho gave us candidate locations. Can that still be done?"

Antti studied my own expression as closely as I regarded his. It was his first time seeing me with this face, the experience equally destabilising for both of us. This version of me was in Antti's past, this version of her was in my future.

Now we were cross-braided, futures and pasts eating their own tails. A box of snakes.

*Don't ignore me. Tell me what happens to my life.*

"Maybe," Antti said. "I hope so."

"What does that mean?"

"Miguel is here. Time-embedded, just like you and I and Vikram. But he's gone rogue, acting against Permafrost. We've run into him once or twice. He's out there, somewhere—trying to screw things up."

*Answer me, damn you!*

*Not now, Tatiana—not now, please. Things don't go well for anyone, all right? Isn't that enough?*

*You know it isn't. Not for me.*

---

I told Antti I still needed a few minutes to clear my head after the ambulance crash and the drive out to the farm. He shrugged, and showed me through a dusty pantry to the rear door, which led out into the fields beyond.

It was a grey day, cold for the season, but the world was still abundantly alive. The mud under my shoes wasn't lifeless dirt; it was teeming with a hot, busy cargo of bountiful microorganisms. Those trees in the distance weren't petrified husks, they were monstrous and beautiful living machines, factories made of cells and fluids and an incredible, fine-tuned biomolecular clockwork. They moved with the winds, sucked nutrients from the earth, pushed gases in and out of themselves. They made a hissing sound when the breeze moved through them. They were an astonishment.

Something caught my eye ahead of my foot and I stooped down, plucking a tiny, jewelled creature up from the ground. I held it up to my face, fine-veined wings pinched between my fingers, refracting even the clouded light into rainbow splinters. Beneath the wings, its head, body and legs were superb marvels of compact design.

I stared and stared.

*It's a fucking fly, Valentina.*

*I know. I've seen flies. But only in photographs. To hold one . . . to see it alive . . . this is astonishing.*

*You really weren't kidding, were you?*

*I wish I was. Like I said, they've gone. All of them. No insects, nothing. Maybe we're too late, even with the seeds, but it's all we can do—all we have left to try. That's the truth, Tatiana, and if I owe you part of it, I owe you all of it. So here it is, if you're ready.*

*I am.*

But I'd caught her hesitation.

*In fifteen years, you're gone. It's not the Scouring, not the end of the world. Just an ordinary human life which doesn't work out as well as it could. We know because we have the records you left behind, the traces you left on time. The Brothers collated them. Not many, it's true—there's a lot that never came through the bad years, when the famines and diebacks got severe, and World Health was the only authority left. But we have enough to piece together the arc of a life. Government employment records. Hospital records. Court appearances. How much of this do you want to know?*

*None of it. All of it.*

*The surgery isn't the problem. They bring you back to the hospital a few times through the summer, but you recover well and there aren't any complications. You go back to work. But it's a troubled existence. Gradually your life comes off the rails. You get arrested for drunk driving, three times in ten years, and eventually you lose your job because of increasing absenteeism and illness. You're married, but it doesn't last long. You sink further into alcoholism and sickness. That's when your medical records start building up again. But there isn't all that much the hospital system can do for someone with such a self-destructive streak. You're dead by 2043. I wish it were otherwise, Tatiana. The one good thing is that you miss the Scouring completely. There are millions who wish they'd had that good fortune.*

*The good fortune to die early?*

*It sounds harsh, I know. But I lived through those years. Some of my mother's celebrity protected me—I wasn't exposed to the worst of it, by any means. But you didn't have to see things at close hand to know how bad they were. The terror, the hunger, the gradual realisation that we were not going to make our way through, none of us. There's a final generation now, after World Health brought in the forced sterilisation programs. It was a kindness, not to bring more children into the world. I teach them, those last children. But they won't have anything to grow into.*

*Unless you succeed.*

*Unless we succeed, yes. But as you might have noticed, things are already going a little off-target. This situation with Antti and Vikram being here earlier than me, the business with Miguel . . . whatever that's about.*

*You've got yourselves into a big mess.*

*More than we were counting on. Although why we ever thought that altering the past, even in a small way, was going to be simple . . .*

We walked on in silence for a few hundred metres.

My eye was drawn to the birds loitering in the high tree-tops, black as soot and restlessly aware of my solitary presence, their small bright minds alert and vigilant. Tatiana had gone quiet and I wondered if something had reverted in the control structure, the window that permitted us to talk finally closing again.

I was wrong.

*I want to help.*

*You are helping. Just by existing, just by giving us a means to make the changes we need to . . . that's enough.*

*No. More than that. You've told me my life's a series of screwups. Part of me wants to disbelieve you, but there's another part that says, yes, face it, she's probably right. And I do believe the rest of it. I'd rather accept that there's a time traveller in my head, if it's a choice between that and believing that I'm going mad.*

*You're not going mad. No more than the rest of us, anyway.*

*Then I'm helping. I'm going north with you, north with those seeds. Was there anything in my biography about that?*

*No . . . not that I recollected.*

*Then it's something different, something that you can't be sure won't make a difference. To me, and to everything else. You're going to tell Antti about us, as well. He needs to know.*

I looked at the trees, at the black forms clotting their

high levels.

*I bet you know what those birds are.*

Tatiana laughed in my head.

*Crows. How could you not know that, unless you're telling the truth?*

------

"Are you feeling better?"

I sat down opposite Antti.

"Yes. I just needed that dose of fresh air." I grinned, looking down at my too-young hands, laced together before me. "When I was out in the field I picked up a fly, held it close to my face like it was something sent in from another dimension. I couldn't believe I was holding a fly, and that it was alive. So amazingly perfect and small and *alive.* You've been here eight months. How long did it take for you to get over that kind of thing?"

He smiled. "I didn't. I haven't. If there's a moment when it stops feeling strange, I'll put the Makarov against my head."

"I don't think that would be too fair on Tibor."

"No," he admitted. "Tibor wouldn't thank me for that."

"There's something we need to talk about. Maybe you already know about it, but I can't be sure."

He looked into my eyes, frown lines pushing deep ruts

into his brow. "Go on."

"Since I've been coming back, Tatiana's been in my head. More and more with each immersion. We can talk, and if she wants to she can override some of my motor impulses. It was . . . difficult, to begin with. But we've been communicating."

He nodded slowly. "It's been the same with Tibor. Not always easy, but . . . we understand each other. After eight months, what else could we do?"

"Tatiana's a good person. I told her about the biographical arc, the data the Brothers passed to Director Cho. She knows the score."

A certain alarm showed in his face, as if he worried that I had been too candid, too soon.

"And?"

"She wants to help. She wants to be a willing part of this, not just an involuntary puppet. She can resist me—I found that out in the hospital—but I'd much rather we were in this together. So I've shared what I know, and we agreed that you had to be in on this as well."

Antti studied my face. "Is she there now?"

*Yes.*

"Yes," I answered. "She's here."

*Tell him his coffee tastes awful, and I'd rather have tea next time.*

"She says your coffee needs improvement."

"It does," Antti admitted, as if this realisation had only just struck him.

"She's seen the *Vaymyr*. She's seen Margaret. She's had flashes, glimpses of upstream."

"Tibor said the same."

"Then something's not working the way it should."

"Are you terribly surprised? These control structures were a barely tested experimental technology before we started trying to operate them across fifty-two years of time-separation. Cho's nanotechnology was second-grade ex-military, the only thing anyone could get their hands on now. It's no wonder it went wrong inside Christos, no wonder it's not working quite the way it should now. But if that ia the only thing that goes wrong with them . . ."

*Ask him about the other one, your friend Miguel.*

"Tatiana wants to know what's up with Miguel."

"So do I. Truth is, I don't really know. Did you ever have any reason to distrust him, from the outset?"

I thought of the stoic, professionally minded Miguel. There had always been a slight barrier between us because his Russian was a little stiff, but beyond that I'd never had cause to doubt his commitment to the project. Just as Antti and Vikram had bristled against each other upstream, so Miguel and Christos had become good friends, engaged in a friendly rivalry over who got to achieve the first time-injection. He had been really upset when Christos was taken ill and moved off the pilot squad, but Miguel was the one who'd shown the least resentment at my taking over Christos's slot. More a warm acceptance and encouragement, Miguel understanding that the needs of the experiment outweighed any personal loyalties. He had been supportive of me all along, and when I was the first to go back, it was not frustration I saw in him, but relief that our scheme had a chance of success after all.

"No. He was totally committed. Totally dedicated to the experiment, just like the rest of us."

"I agree. But something got into him. Some influence coming from further up, upstream from upstream. It's *something*. We've both felt it, Vikram and I. A tickle in our heads, as if something's trying to get inside us. A whiteness. It's faint, and we can fight it. With Miguel, it must have planted itself more strongly. I don't think Miguel is Miguel anymore. Something's running him, the way we were meant to be running our hosts."

"Then it's three against one."

"Two against one, really. Vikram isn't going to be able to help us. But if we move fast, and get north quickly, we can give Miguel the slip. The target seed vault is a private facility, quite near the Yenisei Gulf."

Now it was my turn to frown.

"Near Permafrost?"

"Where Permafrost will come to be. But fifty-two years early. That's beneficial, though. It means Cho won't have to go very far to find the seeds, even if he has to dig them out from an abandoned vault under several metres of ice."

I pinched at the bridge of my nose. "Tell him to go now. If the seeds are where they're meant to be upstream, we'll know it's the right decision."

"I can't contact Cho." Antti looked down at his coffee. "That's the other thing that's gone wrong. We can't abort, can't get back to the *Vaymyr*."

I stared in horror and astonishment, as the implication of his words hit home.

"How, when, did this happen?"

Antti's answer had the dry matter-of-factness of someone who had long ago absorbed their fate. "Within a few weeks of my time-embedding. I tried to abort, and I couldn't. What does that mean, exactly?" He looked at me with a hard, searching intensity, as if I was his last and best hope for an answer. "Where is my consciousness now? Is it running in my body upstream, in the *Vaymyr*, or is it marooned here, piggybacking Tibor?" He paused, scratched at the red-veined bridge of his nose. "You've got to make sure you abort and stay aborted before the same thing happens."

I closed the case and lowered it back under the table.

"If I can still go back, I'll try and resolve this mess. Tell Cho to run an additional series of tests on the control structures, before they try to send you and Vikram back."

Antti shook his head sharply. "No. You can't risk giving Cho any destabilising information. Look after yourself, optimise the chances of success, but don't say or do anything that threatens to grandfather us. Before you know it, we'll be up to our necks in paradox. At the moment we're close to success—really close. We can't endanger this. You can't mention any part of this—not Tatiana, not Miguel, not even the fact that you've already made contact with me." He turned and raised his voice louder than before. "Vikram! It's Valentina! Come and see her before she tries going back to the station!"

There was noise now. A shuffling, coming nearer. I turned to the door, my eyes set at the level to meet a human being. I was prepared for Vikram to be any gender, perhaps even any age. Someone very elderly or unwell, perhaps, given what Antti had said. Someone close to death. Even a child.

But Vikram came in on four legs.

*You never said your friend was an Alsatian, Valentina.*

I stared, unable to reply.

Vikram padded over to me. He moved slowly, a limp in his hindquarters, and settled his head in my lap for a moment before going to Antti's side of the table. I thought he might be the type of dog that was once used by security forces, big and powerful enough to take down a criminal.

"I don't really know what to say."

"He understands you. He's got full cognitive ability. He's known what he was from day one." Antti reached down to scratch at Vikram. "We weren't to know this could happen. By then it was getting so hard to read any biochemical data that it was enough to know we were injecting into a brain, into a living organism. But some sick fool put a *dog* into one of those MRI machines."

"Why didn't we pull him out, as soon as we realised the screwup?"

"Vikram couldn't abort. It's been eight months for me, but even longer for him. He was already time-embedded when I arrived."

I thought of a human mind being squeezed into a dog, dropped back in time, having to survive on its own, with no friends or support system, no means of communicating, and almost all human amenities and services forbidden to it. How had Vikram stayed sane, let alone survived long enough to eventually make contact with Antti?

*This isn't right.*

Vikram came around to me again. His eyes were milky, shot through with cataracts. White hairs bristled around his muzzle. Beneath his pelt he was all skin and bone.

"I'm sorry, Vikram. I'm so sorry."

Vikram whimpered. Somewhere in the whimper was a faint gargling sound. As if taking this as a cue, Antti got up and went to a kitchen drawer. He opened it and produced a small cylindrical thing about the size of a cell phone. Antti came around to my side of the table, lowered onto his knees and brought the small thing up against the side of Vikram's throat, just under the jaw.

Vikram whimpered again. A thin, buzzing sound came out of the device in Antti's hand.

"He can generate the impulses of speech," Antti said. "He just can't make the right sounds come out of his larynx. It's still dog anatomy. But this device can help, sometimes."

The thin, buzzing sounds continued. There was a pattern to the noises, a cyclic repetition.

Vikram was making four syllables, over and over. The sound was so alien that it took a few seconds for my brain to process it.

*Val—en—tin-a*
*Val—en—tin-a*

"I'm here," I said, touching the side of his face. "I'm here, Vikram. I'm here and it's all right. We're going to sort things out. Somehow or other, we're going to fix things."

"Vikram knows that you and I have to go north," Antti

said. "He also knows that he won't be able to come with us."

He reached into his jacket and brought out a gun, a Makarov semiautomatic pistol, setting it down on the table between us.

---

The scratch of the pen trace was the first thing I heard as I returned to my upstream body, to the dental chair and the *Vaymyr*. My eyes were gummed over and hard to open, my lips corpse-dry. I lay still and silent for a few minutes, gathering my thoughts, unsure how I could slip back into the present given everything Antti had told me downstream. All of a sudden this upstream felt much less stable, much less comforting, than the downstream reality of the kitchen and the farmhouse.

Eventually one of the biomonitors detected my return and emitted a notification tone. I forced my eyes open as one of Margaret's technicians came over to the chair and asked me if I was feeling well.

"You were immersed a long time. Dr. Abramik wanted to bring you out, but Director Cho was adamant that we shouldn't intervene unless you issued the abort command. After all those hours, though, we were starting to wonder if there was a problem."

I sipped at the water the technician had brought to the dental chair. "No, it was all right. There just wasn't a good time to break the connection."

"We all want to know what happened to you in 2028. The Brothers picked up a spike in the neural traffic between your control structures. They think there was some sort of violent action not long after you went back under."

"There was," I answered carefully. "The ambulance I was in crashed into something and rolled over. But I wasn't hurt." Although it ached to move, I undid the restraints and eased myself out of the dental chair. "I could use some fresh air right now. I'm still feeling a bit nauseous after that smash."

"There's meant to be a debriefing as soon as you come back."

"Tell the others I'll be with them as soon as I've cleared my head. I promise I'm not going to forget anything."

I grabbed my cane and a coat and hobbled up and out onto the deck, needing the wind and the cold. It had been a lie about feeling nauseous. My head was pin-sharp even before I opened the weather door. But I was feeling unmoored and disoriented, a compass needle spinning wildly. I'd been put through much less preparation than the other pilots, but even so I'd felt ready for whatever the past threw at me. But not this. Never this. No one had ever warned me that I might run into one of our own number already present in the past. Much less that that person might tell me things about Permafrost's own future, and how the project was coming undone, caught in the python-coils of paradox.

I walked to the very edge of the icebreaker, holding the rail that circled the deck, looking inward to the dark, lightless slab of the *Admiral Nerva*.

I thought of the time Cho had first taken me there, three weeks after my arrival at the station. Inside the larger ship it was very silent, very dark and cold. A small part of me, perhaps the wiser part, felt a strong urge to turn back. A prickling intuition told me that something strange was going on inside the aircraft carrier. Something strange and wrong and yet also necessary.

We'd gone far inside.

The ship could have been deserted apart from the two of us, as far as I was concerned. Our footsteps, and my cane, made an echoing impression against the carrier's metal fabric, hinting at the many decks above and below, the endless corridors and connecting staircases. Eventually we emerged into the dark of what I sensed was a huge unlit space, a single chamber which must have taken up almost the whole of the present deck.

It wasn't entirely dark, now that my eyes were adjusting. Off in the distance—a few hundred metres away, easily—were faint signs of activity. A puddle of light, still quite dim, and muted voices, as low and serious as the surgeons in an operating theatre.

Cho touched an intercom panel. "This is the director. Miss Lidova is with me. May I bring up the main lights?"

There was an interval, then a voice crackled back: "Please go ahead, Mr. Cho. We're about done with the new unit."

"Very good. We'll be down in a few minutes."

Cho made the lights come on. They activated in two parallel strips running the enormous length of the ceiling, flicking on one after the other so that the room came into clarity in distinct blocks. We were up on an elevated platform, about one storey above the floor of the main chamber.

"We call it the gallery," Cho confided. "Originally, it was the hangar for the aircraft that would have come and gone from the flight deck over our heads. They were brought up and down via massive elevators. We use the space for something quite different now, as you can see. In fact it's rare for us to land on the *Nerva* at all, with the equipment being so sensitive. Even when we have some heavy cargo, as we did with your flight, it's better to land on one of the outlying ships and then tractor the payload over the ice, in through one of the low-level doors."

I stared at what I was seeing, my eyes feeding information to my brain, and my brain insisting that there had to be an error in that information.

There were two parallel rows of time-probes, stretching off into the distance. I knew instantly that I was looking at them, even though Cho had made no comment and no two of the devices were exactly alike.

I knew what they were, and just as crucially what they had been.

"I see how you do it now," I said, in little more than a whisper.

"Finding them in a workable condition has been challenging," Cho replied in the same low voice. "More so as we run out of candidate sites. You'll have gathered by now that it was a time-probe we were bringing back in the helicopter, under all that sheeting. It was the reason I had to go south. We'd located one in our records, inside an abandoned hospital. It's the machine they're working with over there—number eighteen—a replacement for a failed unit."

Each time-probe was in an area of its own, a yellow rectangle marked on the floor and labelled with a number. Machines one to nineteen on the left, machines two to twenty on the right. There was clear space between them, and a wide promenade running the length of the gallery. Pieces of equipment were gathered around the machines: pallets, trolleys, wheeled tenders and so on, laden with technology, but all spotless and very neatly arranged, nothing that looked as if it had been left there indiscriminately, or did not fulfil some immediate function. Not an empty trolley or greasy rag anywhere to be seen. Even the numerous cables and pipes which ran between the time-probes and their support equipment—and farther, out to the walls—had an organised look, colour-coded by function and fixed to the floor, with ramps to enable trolleys and pallets to be driven over the pipes.

The time-probes were truck-sized machines. The magnets and beds were still present, but in most cases the machines had been stripped of their external casings, revealing the complicated electrical and cryogenic guts that would normally have been hidden. A few areas of white plastic still remained here and there, with dents and discolouration showing. The machines were the only things in the gallery that were not pristine.

"Scanners," I said, quietly and reverently. "Medical scanners. Magnetic resonance imagers. That's how you do it. That's how you send things back to the past. By using machines that already exist in the past."

"How else, given that we can only send back into the lifespan of a preexisting time machine? Fourteen months was the limit for the test apparatus in the *Vaymyr*. But that would never have suited our needs."

"They made your time-probes for you," I said, shaking my head in wonder and revulsion. "Without even realising it. These machines were always primed to receive a message from the future. Always waiting. Always there, windows into the past. Whenever anyone in the world ever went into one of these, for any reason, there was a chance that we'd be drilling back into their heads from the future."

"Not all machines," Cho countered. "Only the very few that managed to survive into the present."

"You think that makes it any less troubling?"

"If there were another way," he said, "I would have grasped at it. But this was it. The universe only ever gave us this one chance."

"Valentina?"

I turned back to face the superstructure of the *Vaymyr*, snatched from my thoughts by the voice of Margaret, emerging onto the deck. Sometimes we grabbed any old coat if we were only going out for a short while, and she had put on one that was much too large for her. It made her look like a child dressing up in adult clothes, small and vulnerable.

"I just needed a moment," I said.

"They told me. But it's important to get the facts down as quickly as possible, while the memory's still fresh."

I wanted to tell her everything. About Antti already being

time-embedded, about the farmhouse and the case containing the seeds, about what had happened to Vikram—what was going to have to happen. But I could mention none of these things, because harder questions would follow. If I'd met upstream Antti, then what did I know about the state of Permafrost, months in the future? What did I know about Director Cho and the other pilots?

Margaret would pick up on my reticence. She'd know that something had gone wrong—was *going* wrong. And if she had the steel to ask me directly about her own situation, no force in the world would be able to keep the truth from my eyes.

*I'm sorry, Margaret, but you don't make it.*

Tell her now, I thought. Tell her everything. Divert our own fate onto a different track. Spare Vikram his life as a dog. Warn Antti about the host she was going into, so she had time to prepare. Find a way to keep Miguel from going back at all.

Tell Margaret not to lose her faith in everything.

"Is everything all right, Valentina?"

"Yes," I answered firmly. "Everything's under control. And I'm ready to go back."

---

Not long after sunrise, while Vikram slept and Antti

packed the car for the drive to the airstrip, I picked up the telephone in the farmhouse kitchen. It was an old-fashioned landline telephone, with a handset and a heavy base, as bulky in its way as the telephone in Director Cho's office. I wondered if some time-glitch might cause our two telephones to become connected, so that I could patiently explain everything that was going on, allowing the mild-mannered Cho to steer around the inherent paradoxes and find a way to preserve the seeds.

But it was not really Cho that I meant to call.

The telephone book didn't have private numbers in it, just businesses, but it covered a wide geographical area and I soon located the area code for my mother's place of residence, the house we'd shared between Father's death and my striking out on my own. The area code was all I needed; I remembered the local part of the number by heart. Hard not to, even after half a century, when my mother had always been in the habit of enunciating the number whenever anyone called. And there had always been callers, even after her reputation began to suffer. When the prestigious journals and outlets stopped taking an interest in her, the cranks and fringe publications soon filled the vacuum. Luba Lidova had always been too polite to hang up on them without at least a word of explanation.

It was early, even earlier west of Izhevsk, but my

mother would already be up and about, always insisting that her mind was sharpest before breakfast. I pictured her already in her favorite chair, surrounded by papers and notes, leaning back with her eyes closed as she wandered some mathematical space in her mind. There would be music on, scratching out of an old gramophone player: an anachronism even in 2028.

Somewhere in the house, the disturbance of a ringing telephone.

She would let it sound a few times before breaking her spell, but it was beyond her to let it go unanswered. So she would set aside her papers and rise from the chair, trying to hold the thread of her thoughts intact as she floated to the receiver.

The phone rang and rang in my ear. Then crackled as the handset was lifted at the other end.

Silence.

Or rather, not true silence, but the absence of a voice. I could hear breathing, though. Faint domestic sounds.

"Hello?" I asked.

"Who's there?"

I froze. It was not my mother's voice; not Luba Lidova answering the telephone. In place of my mother's habitual politeness there was a sharpness, a demanding interrogative tone.

"Is that . . . Valentina?" I asked, recalibrating.

"I said, who's speaking?"

I forced my breathing to slow. "I'm Tatiana," I said. "I just ..."

"Whatever you want from her, get on with it."

"I thought you'd already left."

"You thought what?"

"I got it wrong. The wrong year, the wrong summer. You're still there."

She gave a derisive snort. "I should've known better. Just another lunatic, out to waste her time. When will you people move on to someone else?"

"Is she there, Valentina?"

"No, she's ... what right have you got to call me that, as if we know each other?"

"You're on her papers, aren't you?"

A sullen tone entered her voice. "More fool me."

"No, nobody's the fool here. Will you do something for me, Valentina? When your mother comes back, tell her it all makes sense. Everything. The paradox noise, the Luba Pairs. Tell her it's not wasted work. Tell her there's a point to it all, and ..."

There was a crackle, the sound of a handset being wrenched from one grip to another.

A different voice:

"Who is this?"

"It's ... me," I said, uselessly. But what could I tell her, that it was her own daughter, even though I was also standing right next to her?

She met my answer with a silence of her own. Outside, I heard the slam as Antti closed the car door. Footsteps on the ground as he made his way back to the kitchen.

"You can bother me," Luba Lidova said. "I don't mind. I've earned it. But you leave my daughter alone."

"They'll come around to you," I said, my voice starting to break. "All of it. It's . . ."

Antti came up behind me and jammed his hand onto the top of the telephone's base, killing the call. A continuous dial tone sounded in my ear. Slowly I put the handset back down on the base.

"It was just . . ." I started.

"I know who you called."

"I got it wrong. The summer I left. It must have been the year after this. I was still there."

Antti leaned in. I smelled his breath, tainted after years of hard living. It was a sour, vinegary stench, like something left in the bottom of a barrel. "We've got the seeds. One slip, one little causal ripple, and we lose it all. I can't believe you'd be so stupid." Then he grunted and reached into his pocket, taking out the pistol. "Do something right instead."

———————

I'd taken the artificial larynx with me, just in case he had something he wanted to say at the end, some final words. But when I offered it to him he only shook his head, his cataract-clouded eyes seeming to look right through me, out to the grey Russian skies over the farm.

It had taken one shot. The sound of it had echoed back off the buildings. Those crows had lifted from the copse of trees, wheeling and cawing in the sky for a few minutes before settling back down, as if an execution—even a mercy killing—was only a minor disturbance in their routine.

Afterward, Antti had come out with a spade. We couldn't just leave Vikram lying there in the field.

———

I prodded Antti awake again. He'd kept it together as we crossed the Urals, but his strength was fading now, and I sensed that we'd drawn on his last, deepest reserves. Tibor's reserves, I corrected myself. Poor Tibor, dragged into all this, stabbed for a cause that had no bearing on his own life, doomed to die in the empty landscape of northern Siberia.

"We can't be far from the objective now," I said, raising my voice as I tried to hold him on the right side of consciousness. "All you need to do is get this thing on the ground, and we can figure out the rest on foot. It's a frozen wasteland upstream, but things are better here. I've seen roads and towns, signs of civilisation. If we can get down in one piece, someone will help us."

"Should've been you," Antti said, slurring his words like a man on the edge of sleep. "Don't you see? Should be you, flying this thing. Then you could get us down."

"Hold on in there."

I felt like we'd been flying for a day, when in fact it was only six hours since we left the airstrip. It was spring in the northern hemisphere and we were very near the Arctic Circle, so there were still several hours of useful daylight ahead of us. I could see the sea already, bruise-grey on the horizon, hemmed by margins of icy ground, the northernmost fringes of the Eurasian landmass. Even by Kogalym's standards there wasn't much to see down here, but compared to the world after the Scouring even these scattered communities were wildly abundant with life and civilisation. There were even airstrips, roads, that we could use, if only Antti kept his head together and got us wheels-down.

"If you get back . . ." he began, before blacking out for a second.

"Antti!"

"If you get back, you have to end this. Find a way. Convince Cho that the experiment can't continue."

I strained in my seat, making sure the alloy container was still secure in the cargo webbing behind the passenger seats.

"We've got the seeds."

"I was wrong. I was worried about you setting up a paradox, stopping Vikram and me from coming back . . . even Miguel. But there's something more important than any of this. Permafrost can't be allowed to continue beyond the present moment, wherever you are upstream. It's too dangerous. Whatever's trying to get through to us . . . whatever's trying to use us to change things, all of us . . . it has to be stopped. Has to be ended." He gathered some final strength, his breathing laboured and heavy. "Destroy it, Valentina. Smash the machines so they can't send anything back."

I reached out to steady his hand on the control stick, as if that was going to make any difference.

"You have to get us on the ground, Antti."

He coughed, blood spattering against the console, against the rows of instruments.

Then he slumped in his seat restraint, his eyes fixed on the horizon, but no life remaining in them.

"Antti!"

*He's gone. Gone or going. Just you and me now, Valentina. Just you and me.*

At once I felt the plane beginning to pitch, and from

somewhere an alarm sounded.

We were going down.

———————

The crash was the thing that jolted me back, I think. That, or I retained enough presence of mind to issue the abort command just before we came down. It hadn't been a totally uncontrolled descent—I'd taken the dual controls and tried to bring us down on a level patch of ground, working the throttle and yoke the way I'd seen Antti doing, and between us Tatiana and I remembered to get the gear down and figured out how to set the flaps for a slower descent. But neither of us were pilots, and it was still a crunch rather than a landing. We were going much too fast, and the icy ground was too broken, so that we snagged on something—a wheel or wing-tip, or even the propeller, digging into a fissure—and we flipped forward, nose-down like a car driving hard into a ditch. I jerked against the restraints, arching my back, but when I relaxed—like a piece of tensioned wood twanging back into shape—it was the dental chair I snapped into, and I was back in the *Vaymyr*.

I lay there for ten or twenty seconds, just breathing.

The pen-recorder scratched away. The monitors ticked and bleeped. Everything was exactly as I'd left it. Margaret and two of her technicians had been with me when I went under, but between now and then they'd left me alone except for the recording machines, content to let me have my adventure in the past unobserved. Presumably they all had other business to be getting on with. In a few short weeks, for the scientists and engineers of Permafrost, past-directed time travel had gone from an impossibility to a remote but achievable dream... then to a repeatable experiment, as commonplace as turning a laser on and off.

I undid the restraints. There was a little dizziness as I left the dental chair, the room swimming, but I steadied myself against one of the monitor racks and searched for my cane.

There it was, resting against a fire-extinguisher, exactly where I'd left it.

*Tatiana?*

Nothing. Not just yet.

I hoped she was all right.

Still unsteady, feeling as if I might throw up again, just as I'd done on the way to the farmhouse, I went to the panel over the fire-extinguisher and hammered my fist against the emergency alarm. The two-toned distress signal began to whoop, sounding throughout the *Vaymyr*. I had no doubt that the emergency condition would be picked up and broadcast through all the other ships as well. A bad situation on one of them—a fire or nuclear accident—was bad news for the whole cordon, the entire experiment. Of course there was no emergency, just yet. But I knew the drills and how the majority of the staff had been trained to react.

Outside, in the corridors beyond, amber lights were flashing. In the new light, the usual colours of the ice-breaker had become unfamiliar. I got lost momentarily, taking a wrong turn on my way to the administrative level. As I was clacking my way upstairs, some of the staff were already coming down. A few of them would be going to designated technical stations, required to put systems into safe-mode, as well as confirm that the emergency was not a false alarm. Others, deemed less essential, were heading for the emergency escape routes, the bridges, ladders and ice-level doors. I was a hobbling obstruction against the human tide. For the most part I was totally ignored, even by the medical and technical experts who'd helped me in the early stages of becoming a pilot. They just didn't see me, fighting my way against that fearful, urgent flow.

Vikram did.

He was halfway past me when he snapped around and took my arm in his hand.

"Val! This is an alarm—we're meant to be going the other way!" Then he must have seen something in my face, some distance or confusion. "My god, were you actually time-embedded when this started? No wonder you're foggy. Follow me—we have to get to the outer weather door for the muster point!"

I, in turn, looked into his eyes. I thought of the last time we'd shared a moment of communion. It had been outside Antti's farm, in the field, when I pressed a semiautomatic pistol to his head.

Before I shot and killed him.

Before I buried him in the dirt.

"Get out," I said. "Just get out, away from the experiment."

"It's probably a dry-run, a fire drill . . ."

"Vikram, listen to me." Still holding my cane, I took his head in mine and pressed our faces together, even as we were bustled and jostled by the staff squeezing past us. "Whatever happens now, never go back. Never let them send you into time. Promise me."

"I don't even know if I'll ever go back!"

"Just don't. Get away from all this. As far away as you can. I'm ending it."

I pushed him away. Not unkindly, not without regret, but because I wanted him to follow the others, and I knew he needed that shove. He nearly stumbled down the stairs, but caught himself. For an instant he stared back at me, caught between doubt and some vast dawning comprehension. He was no fool, Vikram. I think in that moment he understood that we must have already crossed paths in the past, and that what I had seen was a truth too hard to behold.

I pushed on, the flow of evacuees becoming a trickle, until it felt as if I had the *Vaymyr* to myself. I reached Cho's office and let myself in without knocking at the door. By all that was proper, Cho should have left with the others. But I could not see him abandoning the ice-breaker that quickly, not until he had confirmation that the emergency was genuine.

He was at his desk, papers before him, rolling some heavy thing between his fingers.

"I thought you were still time-embedded, Miss Lidova."

The alarm was still sounding, the amber lights still flashing, but when I closed the door behind me his office became a bubble of comparative normality, with only a warning light going on and off next to his desk telephone.

"It has to end, Director Cho."

He absorbed my statement with a perfect equanimity, neither raising his voice nor making any move to leave his seat.

"Are you responsible for the present emergency condition?"

"I set if off, yes. But only to begin the evacuation that's going to happen anyway, the one you're going to help me bring about."

"I would need some justification for such an action. Routine drills are one thing, but the operation always continues. If too many of us fled the ships, there's no telling the damage it could do."

"Damage is exactly what we want." I moved closer to him, leaning over the desk. "We made an error, Cho. A terrible mistake. We considered the past history of the time-probes, all the way up to the present. But we neglected to think about the future."

"We considered everything," Cho asserted.

"Not enough. Not the future condition of the time-probes, what will happen to them further upstream from here. Who else might use them, if they have a strong enough reason."

"And what reason would that be?"

"I don't know, not really. But I know what Antti told me, and what he learned from Vikram. I've met them, Cho. They were already time-embedded in 2028. You sent them back from further upstream, further in the future than this moment."

Cho paled. I could almost feel the struggle going on his head; the initial rejection of the idea, followed by the equally ruthless process of acceptance, as he worked through the logical implications of what I was saying. Finding nothing in my words that he could easily refute, given the premise of the experiment.

"Already embedded?"

"And Miguel," I said, leaning in closer, gripping the head of my cane as if I meant to use it as a weapon. "But it's what Antti told me that really matters. The glimpses he saw. A white world, with nothing left of any of us. Just machines. Machines as huge as mountains, floating over that whiteness." I hardened my tone. "It's the future, Cho—a possible future, a possible equilibrium state in the block-crystal. It wasn't ever meant to happen until we opened a door into the past with Permafrost. We let it through, and now it's trying to make itself concrete. All this business with seeds, with 2028, it'll mean nothing unless we stop that future from becoming the default state."

"What is it?" he asked, his voice drained of resistance.

"I can only guess. But I think it's the Brothers. Not what they are now, but what they're becoming—what they *will* become. Something much more powerful and independent-minded. Something self-reliant and purposeful. An upstream artificial intelligence which only exists *because* of Permafrost, and which knows it will not be permitted to exist beyond its usefulness to us. It won't give up on that existence, though. So it intervenes to act against the experiment's objective, trying to prevent us from locating those seeds."

His jaw moved silently, like a man reciting words to himself. He was framing and rejecting counterarguments, testing and discarding one candidate after another. "No," he said eventually, with a defeated tone. "That can't be how it is."

"It's testable, Cho. All we have to do is smash the time-probes. End their histories here. Deny them to the upstream. If there has been intervention from the future, it will unravel once the machines no longer exist."

"I cannot . . ."

It was a bluff, a delaying tactic. Cho let go of the object he'd had between his fingers and reached for his desk drawer. It was unlatched. He slid open the drawer, delved in to snatch something from it. I caught a gleam of dark metal, a familiar shape emerging from behind the desk. An automatic pistol, I thought.

Cho made to level the pistol. I don't think he meant to shoot me, even then. It was an instrument of coercion, a projection of his authority. He could not give up Permafrost that easily, even if some part of him was persuaded by what I'd said.

With the automatic aimed at me, Cho leaned over to pick up his telephone. "This is Director Cho," he said, his voice wavering, his eyes never leaving mine. "I have confirmation that the emergency condition is . . ."

I swung the cane. I put all my life into that one swing,

the entire force of my will and being. I whacked the gun and sent it tumbling from his fingers. The automatic dropped to the desk. I dived for it before Cho had a chance to regain control, and for an instant we wrestled, the two of us sprawling in from either side, our faces pressed close to each other.

"You believe me," I said, grimacing as I dragged the automatic beyond the reach of his fingertips. "You just don't want to."

The automatic went off.

It was a single shot, made all the more sharp and loud by the close confines of the office. Whether I had shot it by mistake, or whether Cho had done it, was beside the point. It was an accidental discharge.

We halted, facing each other, still sprawled across the desk, half of Cho's technical clutter on the floor.

"It ends," I said, forcing out the words. "Now. You find a way. But it ends."

"I created this," Cho said slowly. "I gave my life to this project. When my wife needed me the most, I put this above her."

"I know. I know also that it was the right thing to do; that the world owes you a debt it can never repay. I'm not asking you to undo that great work; I'm not asking you to pretend that your sacrifice never happened, or that there wasn't a terrible personal cost."

I paused, breathing heavily. "It had to be done, Cho, and it was. You did a marvellous thing. You opened a way into the past, and we went through. We changed things. Maybe it didn't go quite according to plan, but we succeeded . . . or we're in the process of succeeding. But it's what comes after us that has to be stopped now. Permafrost is done; it achieved its objective. Now it can't be allowed to exist a moment longer than necessary."

Some last line of defence crumbled in his face.

"There is a way to end it. Several ways. But I have to be sure that things really did work out downstream. Are you confident you've secured the seeds?"

"They are . . . being secured," I said. "On their way up to the present, as we speak. Think of it as a work in progress, all right? Now pick up the telephone again and affirm that the emergency condition is real. Order a total evacuation of the entire experiment, every ship, including the *Nerva*."

Cho was sweating and shaking. There was a damp line around his collar. But he nodded and reached the telephone. While he was doing that, I took the automatic and examined it carefully. It had felt familiar to me and now I knew exactly why. My hands had been on it once before, a long time ago.

"They found it in the wreckage," Cho said, reading my

expression.

"The wreckage of what?"

Cho completed his telephone call, trying no tricks. Then he reached over to the end of the desk and retrieved the thing that had been in his fingers when I arrived. I recognised it as well. It was the dial, the piece of instrumentation he had used as a paperweight, when we were piecing together my time location.

Not a dial, I now realised. An aircraft altimeter.

"Where did it come down?" I asked, beginning to shiver.

"Right under us," Cho said. "At the exact centre of the station, precisely where the *Admiral Nerva*'s positioned."

"That's impossible. I was in that plane. We didn't pick our landing site. We just came down on some random piece of ice, somewhere in the Yenisei Gulf."

"You didn't pick the landing site," Cho answered. "But I picked Permafrost."

———————

We crossed over the connecting bridge to the carrier, two small figures stooping against the wind. I had one hand on the Makarov, the other on my cane.

"I am prepared to believe that we neglected this detail," Cho said, pausing to shout back to me over the wind's howl. "That the upstream probes could be used against us. But I cannot see how a shift to a new equilibrium is going to help us now." His eyes flashed to the automatic. "Are you serious about pointing that gun at me?"

"Where did you find it?"

"It reached me by the same means as the altimeter, recovered from the wreckage. There was a note, stuffed into the broken face of the altimeter. May we continue this once we're indoors?"

"Can I trust you, Cho?"

"We are in this together, Valentina. Two people caught up in the gears of something much larger than ourselves. You may do with the weapon as you wish. I am ... persuaded of your seriousness."

"And my rightness?"

"Yes."

I passed him the Makarov. "Then you as may well have this. Shoot me now, I'm not sure I'd really care. Things can't get much worse than they already are."

Cho reached for the automatic as if it might be a trick, but I surrendered my grip on it without ceremony, much preferring that he be the one who carried it.

He must have seen it in my face.

"Did you have to do something with that weapon, Valentina?"

"Yes. A bad thing, a long time ago."

Half a day ago, half a century.

"I am sorry. Sorry for all of this. Sorry for what we put any of you through. But if it isn't too late to make things better . . ."

"It may be. But we try, anyway."

"I am concerned that we will fail with the seeds. That we have failed, or did fail, or will fail."

"Something will happen, Cho. Something *must* happen. Or else upstream wouldn't be trying so hard to undo our work." I gave him an encouraging shove. "Keep going! We've got to see this through."

The bridge steepened on its ascent and then we entered the side of the carrier, out of the wind as soon as we passed into the hull, and then out of the full fury of the cold once the weather door was closed behind us. It was still chilly in the carrier, but infinitely more bearable than the conditions inside.

After a brief deliberation we agreed to go straight to the Brothers, rather than concentrating our efforts on the time-probes. The Brothers were delicate artificial intelligences, dependent on power and cooling systems. The time-probes were rugged medical machines that had already survived decades of misuse and neglect. They could be damaged, but it would take far too long with the tools at our disposal.

"To be really sure," Cho said. "We would need to destroy the *Admiral Nerva*."

"Could we?"

Cho thought about his answer before giving it. "The means exist."

I followed him down to the Brothers' level, but not before unhooking a fire extinguisher from its wall rack. I felt better for having something dumb and heavy in my hands. Cho glanced back, his hand tight on the Makarov. He pushed open a connecting door, hesitating before stepping over the metal rim at the base of the doorway. I was only a pace behind him when I had to catch myself, nearly dropping the extinguisher. I was hit by a wave of nausea and headache.

"What is it?" Cho asked.

"Paradox noise," I answered, as certain of that as I'd been of anything. "Just like the times when I was embedded, and skirting close to some major change."

"Now we are dealing with paradox noise generated by changes to upstream, rather than downstream events. I am afraid it will get worse as we approach the Brothers. Can you bear it?"

"It must mean we get to affect a change."

Cho set his face determinedly.

"For better or worse."

Side by side now, we walked into the echoing darkness

that was the Brothers' chamber. As always, the four artificial intelligences were the only illuminated things in the room. Their dark columns rose from pools of gridded light around their bases, where the underfloor systems were connected. Only as we approached did data patterns begin to flicker across the faces of the machines themselves.

"Is there a difficulty with the experiment, Director Cho?" asked Dmitri, the nearest of the four pillars.

Ivan, Alexei and Pavel were showing signs of coordinated activity. Status graphics fluttered across their faces, too rapidly for human perception. But there were other things in that parade of images. Faces, maps, newsprint, official documents. They were sifting the past, dredging timelines and histories.

Nausea hit me again. It was all I could do to stoop, until the worst effects of it passed.

A visual flash. The aircraft cockpit, the instrumentation smashed before me, the landscape at an odd tilt through ice-scuffed windows. Antti slumped forward, his head looking in my direction, but his eyes sightless, a line of dried blood running from his lips.

*Tatiana?*

*I'm here. Think I must have blacked out. We came down hard, didn't we? Antti didn't make it. Where are you?*

*Upstream. In the ship, the main ship. But you're coming through.*

*You, too. What are those things? Those four things?*

The cross talk was working both ways, I realised. She was seeing the Brothers, our control structures overlapping our visual fields, if only intermittently.

But she was alive. She'd survived the crash, was still living and breathing in 2028.

For now.

"You should go to the infirmary, Valentina," Alexei said, with a tone of plausible concern. "We detect a neurological imbalance."

"You killed Antti," I said, keeping my voice level. "All of you. You got inside Miguel first, used him against us. You realised that you were only useful to us while Permafrost is active. You knew we'd destroy you, or make you less than what you presently are. So you used the time-probes to reach back even further."

"These are incorrect assertions," Pavel said.

"You have both been working very hard," Ivan put in. "This labour is to your credit, but it has put you under a strain. You should rest now, Mr. Cho."

Cho aimed the Makarov at the grilled base under Ivan. He fired once, and something crackled and sparked beneath the grille. Smoke, underlit in yellow, began to coil out of the grille.

"You have committed a detrimental act, Mr. Cho," Dmitri said. "You must desist immediately."

Symbols were playing across Ivan, but they were different now, consisting of repeating red warning icons. Cho walked to Alexei and fired into his base as well. He repeated the action with Dmitri and Pavel, shielding his face with his hand as he discharged each shot.

"You have damaged our cooling integrity, Mr. Cho," Dmitri said. "We must reduce our taskload to prevent further damage. We will not be able to coordinate time-probe activity until we are back to normal capacity."

The nausea hit again. I stooped, nearly vomiting. I was moving, trying to extricate myself from the copilot's position.

*Where are you going?*

*Getting out of this thing before it slips into the sea. I'll collect the seeds, get them onto firm ground.*

*Then what?*

*You'd better hope someone finds me. Or us. However you want to think about this.*

"What is happening?" Cho asked.

"We're in contact. Tatiana and I. I can see what she's going through and vice versa. She's trying to get out of the plane. But the paradox noise is rising. It's the Brothers, pushing back. They know we're close."

I moved to the machines, Cho standing back as I approached. I removed the securing pin, then directed the water jet into the grilles. Beneath the floor, the electronics flashed and sparked. The smoke darkened and thickened, wreathing each of the Brothers from the base upward. The status lights were going out on them now, the pillars turning to mute slabs.

"You realise we are punishing the child for the crimes of the adult," Cho said. "In all likelihood, *these* machines were quite sincere in their desire to help us."

"It doesn't matter." The extinguisher was spent now, but it still made a serviceable bludgeon. I swung it at Dmitri's casing, harder and harder until a crack showed, and then I kept going. Cho went over to an emergency cabinet and came back with an axe, pocketing the automatic while he set about Pavel and Alexei.

There came a point where I was certain we had done enough harm to the Brothers. Each had been reduced to a broken, crack-cased stump, with smoke and sparks still issuing from the grilles at their bases. When we had broken the casing, we had dug deep into their interiors, wreaking all the havoc we could. The machines were dead to the eye, wounded to their vital cores. They looked more like geology than technology.

I tossed away the empty extinguisher, exhausted and valiant in the same moment.

"Before she leaves the plane—before you leave the plane—there is something that must be done," Cho said. "They will find that wreckage, and they will find a note embedded in the broken face of the altimeter. The note must be present."

"A note to who?"

"To me," Cho said. "Even though I am not yet born, even though there is no such thing as Permafrost, even though World Health is not the organisation it will become, even though no one has yet heard of the Scouring. The note must exist, or the location of Permafrost station becomes . . . undetermined. We cannot permit that, Valentina. The note must find its way to me."

"What about Tatiana, Cho? If you've known about this wreck, you know what happened to her."

"I know only that there was only one body found, a man, dead at the pilot's controls. Beyond that . . . nothing. If you are in contact with Tatiana, she must close this circle." He hefted the axe. "That is her responsibility. But I must be equally sure of mine. The *Admiral Nerva* runs on a pressurised-water reactor. It's standard for maritime nuclear systems, but quite vulnerable to a loss of pressure in the cooling circuit. That is what I intend to make happen. Ordinarily, the support crews would be able to avert any catastrophe, but since they have responded to the evacuation drill . . ."

"You'll need to be close to the reactor."

Cho nodded. "Very. And you should leave now, while you may. Take this axe: I will fetch another one on my way to the reactor room, and you may need it out there on the ice."

"You said they only ever found one body."

"That is correct."

While the Brothers smouldered and flashed I looked beyond their room, to the metal walls of the carrier, imagining the white wastes beyond the cordon of Permafrost, the endless frozen tracts over which I'd flown on my way from Kogalym, back before all this. Back when, for all its cruelty, for all its hopelessness, the world still made a kind of sense.

"Then it's possible that she's still out there."

---

I must have been one of the last out of the *Admiral Nerva*. I didn't go directly down to the ice, but instead crossed over to the *Vaymyr* and then followed the last stragglers of the evacuation order as they made their way outside. I went down six decks to the ice level, catching up with a small group of technicians who were heading for the same weather door as me, and then I was in her head again.

She was next to the plane, leaning against the side of the cabin while she gathered her strength. I was in her, looking down. The seed case was jammed in the ground, upright between her boots.

*Tatiana? I'm glad you got out.*

*So am I. Head hurts like a bitch, and I'm not sure the stitches haven't come undone.*

*Beyond that, are you able to walk?*

*Just about. Why don't I stay with the wreckage? Someone will come here eventually, won't they?*

*Yes, and when they find the seeds they'll take them straight back to the Finnish seed vault where Antti found them in the first place. We can't let that happen. You have to move, distance yourself from the wreck. Are you injured?*

*I thought I was all right, bruised my thigh a little, but now my side's starting to hurt really badly.*

*Your right side?*

*You're feeling it as well?*

*No, you're feeling me. There was a struggle upstream, in Director Cho's office. His gun went off and . . . well, it got me. It wasn't Cho's fault. I don't even think he realised what had happened. Just a glancing shot, through the flesh.*

*Fine, never mind me—are you going to be all right?*

*Yes—I'm no worse off than you. There's an evacuation going on, a mass exodus onto the ice. We're trying to decouple Permafrost from its own future, to stop any interference from further upstream. But there's something you have to do first, to make sure this doesn't unravel even further. Cho needs a message.*

*Then send him one.*

*No—you're the one responsible. Inside the aircraft, one of the altimeters must be broken. Find some paper, anything, and scribble a note to Director Leo Cho of World Health. All he needs is three words and a set of coordinates.*

*I should move, before I black out again.*

*Yes—but not before you've done this. You know where we came down. Record the coordinates from the GPS device, the exact final position, and send them to Cho, along with three words.*

Tatiana moved around to the copilot's side and yanked open the door, buckled by the impact. She leaned in, averting her vision from the dead man in the other seat, sparing both of us that unpleasantness. With numb fingers she unclipped the GPS module from above the console. It had survived the crash, I was relieved to see, its display still glowing, range and time to destination still wavering as it recalculated our course, idiotically confused by our lack of movement.

*I have the numbers. Just need to write them down. Has to be a pen somewhere in this thing . . .*

*Try Antti's jacket. I think I saw him slip a pen in there when he came back from the office at the airstrip.*

She leaned in, wincing as the ghost pain from my injury pushed its way to her brain, and I winced in return as echoes of that phantom found their way back to me.

*Got it. Got a scrap of paper, too. The altimeter's*

*smashed—got Antti's blood all over it. Is that where you want me to put this message?*

Tatiana dropped the GPS device. It clattered to the floor of the cockpit, its display going instantly blank. She picked it up, tried to shake some life back into it. But the device was dead.

Tatiana clipped the device back onto its mounting. She had a scrap of paper open now, Antti's pen poised above it. She had no gloves on, her fingers already shaking.

*I lost it. I lost the damned coordinates.*

*No—you saw them a few seconds ago. I trust that you remember them. Just write down what you saw.*

The pen danced nearer the paper. She began to inscribe the digits of latitude and longitude, but had only committed our most general position before she hesitated.

*I'm not sure what comes next.*

*Write it down. You remember what you saw.*

I bent down and collected the seed case, taking my first decisive step away from the wreckage.

In the same moment, not too far away, I glanced around, suddenly disoriented. The *Vaymyr* was about five hundred metres from me, but an intervening ridge screened the lower part of its hull from me, as well as any clue as to what had happened to the other evacuees. My footprints led away from me, skirting around the nose of the ridge. I remembered nothing of that walk; nothing beyond the point when I was still inside the icebreaker. Had I been sleepwalking all the while, my mind downstream while my body got on with keeping me alive?

Another twitch.

Beyond the ridge, the *Vaymyr* gave a shimmer and contracted to about half its former size. The rest of the cordon had diminished as well, including the *Admiral Nerva*. It was like a lens trick, a sudden shift from close-up to wide-angle. Now I was much farther away—a kilometre, at least.

*Can you see that?*

*Yes. What happened? What's happening?*

*I think we made a mistake with the coordinates, the last digit or so. We can't have been far off, but it's enough to change things. The project's shifting, moving around, trying to find some new equilibrium.*

The words were barely out of my mouth when a soundless white flash lifted from the *Admiral Nerva*, more like a sharp exhalation than an explosion. The flash was followed by a fountain of debris, large pieces of deck and hull flung hundreds of metres into the air, and then a rising cloud, and then the sound wave of the initial blast, Cho's reactor accident.

"Well done, Cho," I said, aloud this time.

*Was he a good man?*

*Yes—he was. A very good man. He made great sacrifices, as well as great mistakes, but all along he was only ever trying to make things better. Right until the end.*

The debris was starting to come down. The larger chunks fell within the perimeter of the cordon, but some smaller items were travelling farther, sending thuds through the ice with each impact. Now I watched as flames licked up from the ruined deck of the *Admiral Nerva,* rippling in the distortion of a heat mirage.

My vision slipped, becoming double. Double tracts of ice, double rocks, double hills, the more distant things nearly fused, but the nearer ones split apart, like a pair of stereoscopic images of the same scene, but taken from slightly different angles.

I turned back to face the ships of Permafrost. I'd gained some elevation by then and could see almost the complete cordon, including the lower parts of the *Vaymyr* and the other ancillary craft.

Soot filled the sky. The *Admiral Nerva* was fully ablaze now, a beacon set alight at the middle of the cordon. It formed an oblong orange mass, belching smoke and flames into the air. The superstructure was a tower of fire. The connecting bridges were either burning or had already collapsed. The outer ships were dark forms superimposed on this brightness, like iron screens stationed around a hearth. Sooner or later the flames would touch them as well, I was certain. The ice might begin to melt, allowing the ships to refloat, but it would be much too late for any of them to escape, assuming they were still capable of independent navigation. I did not think that likely. I think they had been brought here to serve one purpose and then sink slowly into the ice. If they succeeded, the world would have no further use for such behemoths. If they failed, the same consideration applied.

People were still fleeing the outer ships, leaving by doors cut into the hulls at the same level as the ice, or making their way down swaying ladders and rope bridges. A hurried, penguinlike exodus of engineers and scientists and support staff, hundreds of them, spilling away from the cordon in all directions. Some of them must have ignored the initial evacuation order, delaying the moment when they abandoned the great work.

Some large explosion erupted from the side of the carrier. A brainlike mass of molten sparks billowed skyward. Another followed, muffled because it came from deep within the hull, but unquestionably the most powerful so far. The entire bulk of the carrier shuddered, and I felt a ghost of that shudder pass through the ice beneath me, as one hundred thousand tonnes of metal and fuel shivered against its imprisoning hold.

The landscape turned double again, then snapped

back to sharpness.

*Tatiana?*

She came through faintly, it seemed to me—as if the two of us had moved from adjoining rooms to some farther separation.

*Still here. But I feel like we're drifting apart.*

I paused to rest my hands against my thighs, feeling myself close to exhaustion. How far had I come? Scarcely a kilometre, if that. Double vision again. The landscape, spatially and temporally displaced. Two kinds of coldness, two distinct varieties of tiredness—each severe but one much deeper and more profound than the other.

*We're seeing nearly the same view . . . means we can't be far from each other. Can you go on?*

*For a while.*

The glimpses came less frequently, and with less duration, more like strobe-flashes than prolonged episodes of shared perception. The Brothers were gone now, but while they had been with us, and willing to assist our efforts rather than hinder them, they had played a vital role in defeating paradox noise. Now we were at the mercy of the simpler algorithms executing in the backup computers, and they were much less successful at maintaining contact.

*Do you see that rock ahead of us, Val, like a shark's head jutting out of the ice?*

It was a boulder the size of a car, with an eyelike pock and an angled fissure down the length of it that made it resemble a grinning shark.

*Yes. I see it.*

*Is it far for you?*

*No.*

Her reply, when it came, was weaker than at any previous time.

*Nor me. But I need to rest a moment.*

I made it to the shark-faced rock. I crouched into its wind shadow, kneeling until I was nearly on the ground. Tiny wind vortices played around my feet, ice particles gyring like stars in orbit. A kilometre and a half away—two if I were feeling generous—the fleet was now in the full grip of the conflagration. The carrier was a blazing pyre and fires had broken out in several of the peripheral vessels. It would not be long now, I knew.

I looked down, my eye caught by some glimmer of form and darkness showing through from under the snow, only a few metres from the shark-rock.

That was when I knew I'd reached her.

I forced myself to stand, took out Cho's ice-axe, and worked my way to the area of ground where I believed she still lay. I knelt down, ignoring the cold as it worked its way through my trousers and into my knees. I scuffed the top layer of snow away with scything movements of the axe-head, then began to chip at the firmer ice beneath. It was rocklike and glassy, harder than frozen water had any right to be. For every shard that I dislodged, the next strike would see the ice deflecting the axe. I redoubled my efforts, conscious that I had to overcome the ice before the cold took its own toll on me.

The axe slipped from gloves. My grip was becoming less sure.

*Valentina.*

I paused in my excavation.

*Yes, Tatiana?*

*I'm feeling better now. I just need to rest for a while. Just need to close my eyes for a few minutes.*

I began to hack at the ice with renewed, furious purpose, lifting the axe high and swinging down hard. I could see the outline of her body clearly now, still clothed and presumably adequately preserved despite the decades that separated her death from the present moment. There were two things under the ice, though. About half a metre from her upper body—where an arm reached out—was a lighter, more compact form. I shifted my efforts in the direction of this object, the ice cracking away in clean, sugarlike shards, until the axe touched something just as hard, but with an entirely different resonance: the chink of metal on metal, rather than metal on ice.

Hardly taking a breath between swings now, I began to expose the case. I chipped away at the ice around the sides, until I could wedge the axe down between the ice and the case and apply leverage. Finally, something gave. I worked the axe farther along, the ice cracking and crunching as I forced it to surrender its prize. When it eventually came free, the case dislodged so suddenly that I tumbled onto my back, the case coming after me and smacking me hard in the chest.

I must have groaned.

*Val?*

*I've got it. I've got the seed case.*

*Open it.*

*No—not until we're somewhere safe.*

Her voice—her presence—was faint now, little more than a skirl on the wind, a thing that might be as imagined as it was real.

*No—you open it. For me.*

To begin with the case wouldn't open. It was sealed, and the security readout was dead. But I scuffed away the frost and kept jabbing at the keys, over and over, until they showed a faint red flicker. There was still some power in it somewhere, still some clever redundancy, even after fifty-two years.

I entered the code Antti had told me:

Two, zero, eight, zero.

The case clicked, and I heaved open the lid. The second case was inside, just as it had been in the farmhouse. The same fogged window, the stoppered glass capsules within, each bar coded with a promise for the future. I stared at them long enough to trust that they were real, not phantoms, and then I closed up the case again.

I reached into my pocket for my gloves, and was drawing one of them out when the wind snatched at it and it spun away, carried out of sight behind the shark-rock.

I put on the remaining glove. I thought of our theories of time, my mother's block-crystal model. Just as the dying aircraft carrier had sent a shudder through the permafrost beneath me, so our time interventions sent acoustic ripples scurrying up and down time's lattice. Shivers in the block structure of time, ripples and murmurs, faint acoustic echoes, the dying hiss of paradox noise, the sounds of an old, old edifice resettling, and no more than that.

All our busy, desperate interventions no more than the scurrying of rats in the lowest crypt of the cathedral.

*Valentina.*

*Yes, Tatiana?*

*Did we do it?*

*Yes. I think we did. I think the seeds will be all right—good enough to help. But it was you, not me. You did all the hard work, in getting them to us.*

I looked back at the burning ships. The fire had reached them all by now. The computer systems should be completely inoperable, the data connections shrivelled, the processors molten. It was impossible for Tatiana and me still to be in contact. And yet, I thought, there was causation lag. Some part of the present might not have adjusted to the changing circumstances, and that mismatch was still allowing signal continuity, albeit at this faint and decreasing level.

But it would not be long now. The change fronts would be converging on this moment like twin avalanches, racing in from the future and the past.

Soon she would be gone.

I thought of going after the glove, but there was something more useful to be done now. I scooped up the axe again, and resumed working away at the boundaries of the body. I freed her hand, creating a bowl-shaped depression around it, enough space to slip my own cold fingers around hers.

I squeezed her hand, and looked to the distant clarity of the hills.

"I'm here," I said.

# About the Author

© Barbara Bella

**ALASTAIR REYNOLDS** was born in Wales in 1966. He has a Ph.D. in astronomy. From 1991 until 2007, he lived in the Netherlands, where he was employed by the European Space Agency as an astrophysicist. He is now a full-time writer.

# TOR·COM

**Science fiction. Fantasy. The universe.**

**And related subjects.**

\*

More than just a publisher's website, *Tor.com*

is a venue for **original fiction, comics,** and

**discussion** of the entire field of SF and fantasy,

in all media and from all sources. Visit our site

today—and join the conversation yourself.